BEDTIME STORIES

FOR KIDS

Unforgettable short tales with Ralph and his sweet friends that help your children fall asleep (it includes Christmas stories)

Book 1

Gordon Green

Gordon Green is a respected primary school teacher with decades of teaching experience. Through the years, he has developed many techniques to make his lessons as stimulating as possible. This helps to capture the attention of his students.

With his bedtime stories, he attempts to make his readers more aware and respectful by enriching their imagination and creativity. Each chapter has a special moral lesson, though they are conveyed in a way that helps children to learn values without feeling they are being preached to.

A special thank you to Michele, a 12-year-old boy, who is the artist responsible for the following drawing in the book. Although he does not attend a professional drawing school, his skills are remarkable and noteworthy.

Table of contents

Chapter 1: A Dog Named Noodle

It was the first morning of the first week of summertime. The sun peeked over the trees in the park across the street, bathing everything in a warm glow of light. The traffic raced by, with red cars and black cars and blue cars all filled with people driving hither-and-thither and honking at each other. But 7-year-old Ralph didn't notice any of this. Ralph was lonely. All his friends from Carberry Street had gone away on vacation - even his best friend Sam, who *never* went away.

Ralph sat on the front steps of his house watching the city come to life around him. A man and a woman meandered by, holding hands. Two men talking very quickly hurried by, each talking to the other, but neither listening. Even frumpy old Mrs. Smith from down the street, he thought, had her cat, as she ambled by with the brown tabby creature in her arms, her long patchwork skirt trailing behind her. It seemed that absolutely *everyone* had someone - except for Ralph.

Ralph's mother came out onto the step. "What's wrong, Ralph?" she asked. She looked surprised at his downcast face.

"I'm bored!" Ralph told her. "I don't have anyone to play with at all!" As hard as he tried, he couldn't stop a single tear from running down his face. Then another escaped. And another.

"Oh, Ralph!" His mom sat down next to him. "There are times in your life when you are going to be alone. You will have to learn to accept that." She brushed her brown hair back out of her face. "Find something to do. It's going to be a long summer if you just sit and feel sorry for yourself. Why don't you go read a book?"

"Don't want to," answered Ralph, a bit sulkily. His mother just didn't understand.

Mom didn't say anything else. She just looked at him sympathetically, then put an arm around his shoulder for a moment. She got up and walked back into the house, leaving Ralph sitting by themselves... alone again, he though self-pityingly.

A while later, while Ralph was helping Mom wash the dishes, Dad came home. Dad worked at a factory down the street, so he often left the house when it was still dark and arrived home late in the morning when the sun was out.

Dad noticed Ralph's tear-stained face and gave him a hug. "Rough day, Ralph?" he asked. Ralph saw Mom and Dad exchange a look over his head.

A few minutes later, Ralph went to lay on his bed by himself. He didn't feel like doing anything at all. But then Dad came into the room. "Come on, Ralph!" he said cheerily. "We're going on a road trip!"

Ralph was excited! Road trips were fun! Road trips meant ice-cream at the shop down the street, or sometimes even jaunts to the gymnasium to play basketball! Where could they be going?

Ralph followed Dad out of the house. They got into the family's black car and drove across town. Dad pulled the car through the gates of a large building that Ralph had never seen before. Suddenly, Ralph heard a strange sound. Was that a dog barking!?

They passed a big green sign that read, "Sagaro Animal Shelter." Ralph felt a huge grin split his face! Could they be getting a dog?

Ralph had been wanting a dog for what seemed like forever! But every time he asked, Mom and Dad had said, "Not NOW, Ralph." But maybe "NOW" had finally come!

Dad smiled at him. He parked the car near the front door of the yellow building. They walked inside. Ralph couldn't hold his question inside anymore! The words spilled out, falling over each other. "Dad, are we here to pick out a dog!?"

Dad grinned, suddenly looking like a little boy himself. "Your mom and I decided it's time you had a pet. And," he added, straightening his glasses, "I was about your age when I got my first dog! Dogs really are a man's best friend," he added, tousling Ralph's hair in an affectionate way.

Ralph ran into the first room he saw. There were dogs in cages. He saw big dogs and small dogs, black dogs and white dogs. He saw dogs that looked happy, and other dogs that looked sad - like the way Ralph had been feeling earlier that day, before they had come here. There were dogs with loud barks, and dogs with shrill barks! Ralph even saw a dog with three legs, and another without a tail! Some dogs jumped excitedly against the bars, while others sat quietly in their cages.

They saw dogs of all sizes and colors. Ralph wished he could take every one of the dogs' home with him!

"What about this dog?" Dad asked. He was pointing to a huge black dog with long, thick fur.

Ralph hesitated. "That dog's too big."

Ralph pointed to a tiny little dog with a curly tail. "What about this dog, Dad?"

Dad hesitated. "I think that dog is a little too small, son."

Ralph's dad walked out of the room for a moment. Suddenly, Ralph saw a small brown dog looking at him. He went over to its cage. The dog cocked its head, looking up at him with soft brown eyes. Its body was long and thin.

The sign on the cage read "Name: Noodle."
Underneath that, in small red letters, it read "Male Dachshund." Ralph knew that meant the dog was a boy.

Ralph smiled at the dog. "Hello, Noodle! Come here boy!"

Noodle's response was immediate! He began to wag his tail so hard, it looked like it might fall off! The dog's whole body wiggled! Ralph just knew this was the dog for him.

Ralph started to walk away to go find Dad. He looked back at Noodle, who looked disappointed to see him go. His tail dropped. "I'm just going to find my dad!" he tried to explain to Noodle, who wagged his tail again hopefully. Ralph could have sworn the dog nodded to him!

Dad was in another room, talking to a lady who, Ralph thought, looked very nice. She was smiling as Dad told her exactly the kind of dog they wanted. She wore a badge that said "Sagaro Animal Shelter-Volunteer."

"No, wait Dad!" cried Ralph. "I found the perfect dog for us! His name is Noodle."

"Noodle!" exclaimed the lady. Her smile became even wider. "That's exactly the dog I was going to suggest to you! Noodle is such a good dog." She disappeared into the back room and returned with a leash. "This is for you to use to walk the dog," she explained to Ralph. But Ralph already knew. He had seen people walking dogs around his neighborhood using these.

All three of them walked back to Noodle's cage together. When Noodle saw Ralph coming, he went into a frenzy! He rolled around on the floor of the cage, his short legs waving in the air. Little yipping sounds flew out of his mouth in short breaths. Ralph's father laughed out loud. "I'd say that's your dog, Ralph!"

The nice lady clamped the leash on Noodle and handed the other end to Ralph. Ralph and his dad went through a pair of double doors into a sort of outdoor courtyard outside the building. There was a bubbling fountain. They walked Noodle around the courtyard. The dog seemed ecstatic to be outside. He sniffed the grass and seemed interested in all the different smells.

"He's probably tired of being stuck inside all the time," Ralph said to Dad. "We *have* to take him home." Ralph had never wanted anything so badly in his life. What if Dad said no? But Dad's beaming smile told him all he needed to know.

"Want to go home with us, Noodle?" asked Ralph. Noodle looked up, his eyes twinkling. Ralph could have sworn the dog was smiling at him.

As they left the shelter, Dad looked at Ralph. "There's one more place we need to go, Ralph." He went on "There's much more to having a dog than just playing with him all the time. Noodle needs to be taken care of, and since he's your dog, you need to be the one to do it."

Ralph felt very grown-up to hear Dad talking to him like this. "Yes, sir!" he said proudly. Ralph knew he could learn to take care of Noodle himself!

Dad pulled the car up to a store. The sign over the door said "Pets Unlimited." Another, smaller sign in the front window said, "Pets allowed." Ralph was excited. He knew that meant that Noodle was allowed to go into the store with them!

Dad led Ralph to an aisle labeled "Dog food." They chose a large bag of food. Next, Dad chose a box that said, "Dog Treats." Finally, they walked to the other side of the store to get Noodle a new collar.

"What color do you think we should get?" Dad asked Ralph.

Ralph considered. He pulled an electric blue collar from the rack. Somehow, it seemed to have as much energy as Noodle, he thought! "Can we get the matching leash, Dad?" Ralph asked, having spotted a leash of the exact same color on a nearby rack. Dad nodded his assent.

"Aren't you going to ask Noodle if he likes it?" asked Dad. The quick grin that lit up his face showed Ralph he was teasing. Ralph grinned back. "What do you think, Noodle? Do you like it?" asked Ralph. Noodle looked up at them with his limpid brown eyes. He gave a definitive "Yip!"

"I'd say that's a 'yes!' said Dad.

When they arrived home, Mom was waiting for them. She gave Ralph her gentle smile. "This is Noodle!" Ralph told her.

"Welcome home, Noodle!" Mom said. She opened the box and gave the dog a treat! "Arf!" said Noodle, but his doggie voice was muffled, since he was gobbling down the treat at the same time.

Dad pulled a plastic measuring cup out of the kitchen cabinet. "You can have this one to use when you feed Noodle," he said to Ralph. Next, he pulled out a silver bowl. He showed Ralph exactly how much food to put in the bowl. "You need to feed him twice a day - once in the morning and once at night."

Ralph took the food and put it in the bowl. He set it on the floor. Noodle, who had been walking around the room sniffing at everything, instantly ran to the bowl and fell to eating. He didn't stop until he had eaten every morsel!

Ralph swelled with pride. He had someone to take care of!

"Now," said Dad, "It's important to walk a dog several times a day. A dog needs exercise!"

Ralph pulled the collar and leash from the pet store bag. At the sight of them, Noodle jumped on the couch and began rolling around, waving his paws in the air with excitement. "I think he knows what it is, Dad!" laughed Ralph.

They walked Noodle around the block. Several of the neighbors stopped them to ask about their new dog. "Hello, Noodle!" they all said. Noodle licked their hands and said, "Yip! Yip!"

They went home and ate dinner. Ralph took his bath and brushed his teeth. Noodle followed closely at his heels.

When It was time to go to sleep, Noodle jumped into bed with Ralph. He snuggled up next to his new master's leg as though he'd been sleeping there forever. The dog gave up a contented little sigh as he went to sleep. Every so often, Ralph saw Noodle open up his eyes for one last look, as though to make sure Ralph was still there.

Just before Ralph drifted off to sleep, he heard Mom enter the room. She smiled upon him and Noodle. "No one is ever lonely as long as they have someone - or something - to take care of," she said, hitting upon a very important truth. She kissed him goodnight. Then she switched off the light and left the room.

And Ralph just knew neither he nor Noodle would be lonely anymore.

Chapter 2: The New Girl

The family's minivan turned down the busy street. The wind whipped through Emily's long, blonde hair as she gazed out the van's open window. She just caught a quick glimpse of a sign that said "Carberry Street" as the family's van rolled past.

Dad stopped the car. "We're finally here!" He announced cheerfully. Dad had a habit of announcing *everything*. Usually, Emily found it endearing. But today, she was not happy.

They were moving to a new town where Emily didn't know anyone at all. The fear made her stomach clench so that it fluttered a little. She shifted a little in her wheelchair. She just knew she wasn't going to make any friends.

Not that she'd had many friends at home anyway. The only person who ever wanted to play with her was her cousin Bobby, and that was only because he sometimes came to visit with his parents. But she and Bobby didn't go to the same school - he and Aunt Susie and Uncle Bruce lived far away. They lived so far that when Emily and her family wanted to visit them, they had to drive for two hours in the car! But, Emily thought, Bobby was the closest thing she had to a friend.

Most other children didn't know how to treat her because she was in a wheelchair. Some kids laughed at her; they didn't seem to know what else to do. Others looked like they felt sorry for her, but didn't really know what to say. They didn't understand that she was just like them. Only her outsides looked different.

She felt sad a lot, though. Other kids her age seemed to be happy most of the time. Back before the car accident, when she had been just like them, she had been happy too.

Well, she thought, at least her family had moved here at the start of summer. This meant she wouldn't have to go to school for a few months. Maybe by the time school started, she would be used to living in the city.

Emily's tired-looking mother came around and opened the back door of the minivan. She pulled out a special ramp. She put it into place so she could help Emily roll her wheelchair down onto the sidewalk.

Emily looked around. This new city didn't *look* very scary, she thought. It just looked big. Much bigger than the little farm where her family had lived up until now. There were a lot of cars driving by. Emily noticed that everyone seemed to be in a hurry.

As Emily's mother pushed her across the sidewalk, she heard someone shout, "Noooooooodle!!!!" She looked down to see a brown blur of a dog headed right for her wheelchair! A chubby red-headed boy came careening around the corner after it. Just in the nick of time, the dog skidded to a stop. It looked up at her, panting. She saw a pair of lively brown eyes before the dog jumped suddenly, unceremoniously, into her lap! Emily's mom cried out in surprise. Before Emily knew it, though, she herself was giggling and couldn't stop. Startled, she realized that she hadn't laughed this hard since before she'd found out they were moving.

The boy skidded to a stop next to her, halting just as quickly as his dog had. He looked like he didn't know whether to laugh or be embarrassed. He looked relieved to see that she was laughing. "We just got him a few days ago," he told her. "He likes to run, so he keeps getting out of the house. He goes around our legs when we open the door. Then he takes off down the street!" He added boisterously, "He has a lot of energy!"

Emily continued to smile as she stroked the dog. Apparently, the dog liked it since he made no move to get off her lap. "His name is Noodle?" she asked. He nodded yes. "Hello, Noodle."

"I have a dog named Ruby," Emily told the boy. "My uncle is bringing her tomorrow." Her little white dog had stayed with Uncle Jack for a few days while the family was moving. "Would you like to have a new friend, Noodle?" she asked. Noodle looked up at her with his sparkling brown eyes. "Arf!" he confirmed. They all laughed together.

This boy looked nice, Emily thought. When the boy smiled, it made her want to smile too. And this boy didn't look like he would be afraid of *anything*. Also, Emily noticed he looked at her face the whole time he talked to her. He did not even seem to notice that she was in a wheelchair. Emily wished a boy like this would want to be friends with *her*.

"Ralph!" Emily heard a woman's voice call. The boy snatched up the dog. He turned around and sped off towards the voice. "Bye!" He tossed back over his shoulder. Emily guessed the lady calling Ralph was his mother.

"What a nice boy!" said Emily's mother. She picked Emily up and carried her up the steps, leaving the wheelchair at the bottom. Emily knew Dad would fold it and bring it up later - he always did. "It would be nice if you made some friends in the neighborhood," Mom added, as she carried Emily through the door of their new house.

"That boy *was* nice," said Emily. Voicing what she had been thinking to her mother, she said "He didn't even seem to notice I was in a wheelchair!"

Her mom smiled sympathetically at her, then looked thoughtful. "Emily, there are a lot more people in the city. It may not be a big deal to him. Maybe he knows other children who are in wheelchairs, too!" Emily was startled. Imagine a place where children in wheelchairs were common! The scared feeling in Emily's stomach eased a bit, and she found she was beginning to feel better. "Talking to him was like having a friend, Mom!" Emily said, a little wistfully. And she couldn't help adding, "And his little dog was so cute!"

Later that night, as Emily was going to sleep, she wondered if maybe living in the city wasn't going to be as bad as she had thought.

The next morning, Emily sat at the table eating her eggs and bacon. From where she sat, she could see out the window. Suddenly, she saw Ralph walk by! He had Noodle on a leash. He stopped in front of the window to allow Noodle to sniff the bright red fire hydrant in front of their house.

Dad came into the kitchen. "Hello, Pumpkin!" he said, stooping down to drop a quick kiss on her head.

"Good morning, Dad," said Emily, as she munched on a piece of bacon.

Dad looked out the window to see what Emily was watching. "Is that the boy you and Mom met yesterday?" he asked.

"Yes!" Emily answered. "I like him. I wish I had a friend like him."

Dad sounded surprised. "Well, why don't you make friends with him then?"

Emily rolled her eyes. Parents could be so … dense sometimes, she thought. "I'm afraid he wouldn't want to be friends with me. Because of my wheelchair." Dad was silent for a moment, so she went on, "There are lots of kids he could be friends with who *aren't* in wheelchairs. Why would he want to be friends with someone who is?"

Emily's dad came over and sat down at the table next to her. He seemed to be thinking hard about what to say. "Emily, when you are afraid of something, you need to find a way to <u>overcome</u> that fear."

Emily was puzzled. "What does that word mean, Dad? 'Overcome?'"

Dad was thoughtful. "It means to get over something. So, when you are afraid of something, you need to find a way to not be scared of it anymore."

He continued, "When you are afraid of doing something, you should always decide if it's a good fear."

"For example, Emily, would you want to put your hand into a lion's mouth?"

Emily looked at him, startled. "Of course not!"

Dad smiled, running his fingers through his short hair. "Right answer! You might have a fear of doing that, but that's a good fear. That's a fear that will keep you safe."

"On the other hand, though, being afraid to try to make friends with Ralph is *not* a good fear. Because you could be missing out on having a nice friend. So that's the kind of fear you need to overcome. And, Em... What's the worst thing that could happen?"

Emily thought for a moment. "He won't want to be my friend?"

Dad stood up. "Exactly. But at least you will have tried." He took his car keys off the small gold hook by the front door. "And, Pumpkin... even if Ralph doesn't want to be friends, you will have overcome your fear just by trying to make friends with him. Does that make sense to you?"

Emily thought about it for a moment. "I think so!"

Dad opened the door. "The next time you see Ralph, I want you to try to make friends with him. Promise?"

She smiled. "OK, Dad!"

Later that day, while Emily was watching television, she heard a knock on the door. She listened curiously. "Hello!" she heard her mother say, and she heard a boy's voice answer.

She wheeled her chair into the kitchen. There stood Ralph! "Where's Noodle?" she asked curiously.

Ralph grinned at her. "I was going to see if you wanted to play with me. After he jumped on you yesterday, I thought maybe I'd leave him home today."

Mom said, "That was very considerate of you, Ralph!"

Emily said, "I didn't mind, though. You can bring him anytime. I love Noodle!"

Ralph went on, "I'm so glad you moved in! All the kids on the street are on vacation. I haven't had anyone to play with... well, except for Noodle," he added.

Emily was surprised. She had never thought of herself as someone another kid would be excited to play with. She smiled.

Emily remembered what she had talked about with Dad that morning. Well, if she was going to try to overcome her fear, she might as well just say it and get it over with, she thought. "Ralph, do you want to be my friend?"

He shrugged. "Sure, I do. Why wouldn't I?"

"Some kids don't want to be my friend because I'm in a wheelchair," she told him.

Ralph didn't look bothered. "So what? There's a bunch of kids at my school in wheelchairs. Well... actually, like 3 or 4, anyway," he said, considering. "Why would I care about that?"

Dad had been right! Emily couldn't wait for him to get home later so she could tell him so. And now, once she had talked about her fear, it even seemed a bit silly. She would tell Dad that too.

She and Ralph played board games and listened to music all afternoon. Mom even took a break from her housework to come and sit with them for a while and play with them! Ralph told them about some of the other children who lived in the neighborhood. They all liked to play together, and Emily could play with them too, he said, if she wanted to.

Early that evening, Dad came home. He looked thrilled to see Ralph there. "Why don't you stay for dinner with us, son?" he asked. "We're ordering out for pizza!"

Ralph left shortly after dinner, but only after promising to return the next day. Right before bedtime, Uncle Jack showed up with Emily's dog Ruby.

"Ruby!!" shrieked Emily with excitement. She had missed her dog so much! Ruby hurled herself into Emily's lap with short, happy barks! Emily stroked her dog's soft, white fur and felt that today had been a perfect day.

"I have a new friend for you to meet tomorrow, Ruby! His name is Noodle," she told the dog. Ruby grinned her big dog grin and snuggled closer.

As Emily went to sleep that night, she thought how happy she was that she had learned to overcome her fears! The future didn't seem so scary to her now. She smiled sleepily as Ruby licked her face goodnight.

Chapter 3: Choices

Ralph was bored. He was sitting in front of the TV, but he wasn't really paying attention to it. Noodle lay snoring at his feet.

He's been playing with his new friend Emily every day, but she had gone away to visit family for the weekend. None of his friends on the street were back from vacation yet. It was Friday, so Dad was at work. Mom had gone to her book club. Ralph was alone except for his babysitter, Ayesha, and she would barely even look up from her phone to acknowledge him. Ralph needed something to do. Maybe, he thought, I will go over to the park and walk Noodle.

He stood up and stretched. Noodle stood up and stretched too! He gave Ralph an expectant look. Where are we going? he seemed to be asking.

Ralph grabbed the leash from its rack behind the basement door. Noodle began to run excitedly in circles. Ralph laughed out loud. Noodle always went into a tizzy when he saw his special blue leash being pulled out! His dog knew that meant it was time for a walk.

Ralph clipped the leash on Noodle's matching collar. "We're going to the park!" He called to his babysitter. She grunted in return. The boy and his dog walked out the front door together. The park was across the street. As he had been taught, Ralph stopped and looked both ways, making sure there were no cars before crossing.

They had only been walking for a few minutes when Ralph saw Johnny Colantuoni hanging out by the tennis courts. Johnny was an older boy that had gone to Ralph's school last year. Next year, though, he would be in middle school. Johnny lived in another neighborhood. Ralph wondered what he was doing here.

Johnny beckoned to Ralph to come over. Ralph hesitated. He didn't like the older boy all that much. He was, as Ralph's mom would say, "rough around the edges." Sometimes he could even be a bully! However, the older boy was considered to be one of the "cool kids" at school. "Oh well!" thought Ralph. "I'll just go over there for a minute."

Johnny scowled at Ralph in greeting. "When did you get a dog?" he demanded.

Ralph shifted uncomfortably. He felt intimidated already, but he didn't really have a good reason to leave yet. "A few weeks ago," he replied.

Johnny looked bored. "Let's go somewhere else," he said. "There ain't nothing to do." He spit out a curse word.

Ralph was shocked by the curse word, and he was tongue-tied. He knew he should speak up and say "no;" after all, he had only told Ayesha he was going to the park and nowhere else. But he didn't want to make the older boy mad. Besides, it made Ralph feel important to be hanging around with an older kid. Wait until Sam comes back from vacation! he thought. He couldn't wait to tell his best friend that Johnny had wanted to hang out with *him*. None of the cool kids ever wanted to hang out with Ralph at school.

Johnny walked down the street towards the bicycle shop. Ralph followed, with Noodle walking closely at his heels. They passed the bakery. Ralph's stomach growled. It had been a long time since he'd eaten breakfast, he thought, and the bread smells wafting out were making his mouth water.

As they passed the bakery, Ralph waved at Mrs. Johnson, the nice lady who worked behind the counter there. She smiled and waved at Ralph, but then frowned when she saw that he was with Johnny.

Johnny went into the bicycle shop, leaving Ralph standing alone outside with Noodle, who wandered happily up to the people walking by. Some of them ignored him, but many people stopped to pet Noodle. "What a cute dog!" they said. "Thanks!" said Ralph proudly. "Arf!" responded Noodle.

It seemed to Ralph that ages had gone by since he left home, although in reality it had been only a few minutes. He had a sudden longing to go home, where people didn't scowl or curse. He remembered how he had been tired of sitting around the house watching TV this morning. Now he would do anything to be back in that safe, comfortable environment.

Johnny wandered back out of the shop and gazed down the street. "Let's go over there," he said, pointing across the railroad tracks. Ralph's stomach clenched into a knot. Ralph knew the rules his parents had laid down for him. He was allowed to play anywhere in the neighborhood on this side of the railroad tracks, but he was not allowed to cross them.

Johnny took a cigarette out and lit it. Ralph gaped at him in surprise. "What a baby you are!" Johnny burst out, disgusted. "Haven't you ever seen anyone smoking before?"

Ralph felt the tears start to burn behind his eyes. He wanted to say he had just never seen another kid smoking. His Uncle Jack smoked cigarettes, after all. But it was something only grown-ups were supposed to do.

Johnny didn't even seem to notice him anymore. He walked away, not paying attention to Ralph at all.

As he walked away, Ralph looked at the older boy's Nike basketball shoes. Ralph wished he could have shoes like that. Ralph's mother got his shoes from the discount store.

Ralph followed. He didn't want to, but he didn't want Johnny to tell everyone he was a baby, either. He wanted the older boy to like him.

They crossed the railroad tracks; first Johnny, followed by Ralph, with Noodle trailing behind on his leash.

"I came all the way over here to see Jared," said Johnny, mentioning one of the older boys on the street. "But he's not home." He frowned.

"They're on vacation," Ralph volunteered. He sometimes played with Jared's younger brother. Johnny scowled, as though Jared being on vacation had been done on purpose to make him mad.

"The last time I was over here the old man who owns this store got mad at me," said Johnny calmly. Then, without warning, he picked up a brick and threw it at the window on the side of the store. To Ralph's shock, the window broke, shattering into tiny pieces! Johnny laughed. He took off running down the railroad tracks.

Ralph just stood there, shocked. Noodle gave a yelp of surprise, perhaps frightened by the noise of the window breaking. Ralph picked his dog up to comfort him. "It's ok, Noodle!" he said. Noodle whimpered. The store owner came out shouting. Ralph felt like he was in a bad dream. It was as though his predictable little world had been turned upside down and inside out.

"You kids!" screamed the owner. He looked surprised to see Ralph standing there. Suddenly, he looked at something over Ralph's shoulder.

Ralph turned to see what he was looking at. He turned right into his father's disappointed face.

Dad looked as though he were totally at a loss for words. "Ralph!? Did you break that window? And what are you doing over here?" he added as an afterthought, gesturing angrily to the railroad tracks.

Ralph could take no more. He burst into tears.

Dad looked at him, shocked. The store owner glowered at him, angry.

"I didn't break the window!" Ralph sobbed. "He did!" He pointed at Johnny, who was still running away along the tracks.

The store owner took one look and understanding dawned on his face. "Oh! That kid." He added, "I just had to run him out of my store the other day. He tried to steal something."

Ralph turned again to look at his father. Dad looked a little less angry - but he still didn't look happy. He looked like he still didn't quite understand what had happened. "Ralph, let's go home," he said shortly. "Apologize for the window."

"I didn't do it!" bawled Ralph. "...But I'm sorry that it happened anyway?" he added, as his father glared at him.

Dad marched Ralph back over the railroad tracks toward home. How happy Ralph was to see the brick townhouse with the white trim! He could not remember ever being gladder to see it.

Dad sat Ralph down at the table. "Tell me everything."

Ralph did, starting with his decision to take Noodle to the park and ending with Johnny throwing a brick through the store window.

Ralph's dad listened. As the story went on, he started to look a little less angry.

When Ralph had finished, Dad said, "Ralph, you made quite a few bad choices today." He paused, staring at the ceiling as though he wasn't really seeing it.

"In life, Ralph, making bad choices can lead to very bad consequences. What do you think was the first bad choice you made today?"

"Leaving the park with Johnny?"

Dad considered. "You should always keep good company, Ralph. That means," he added, as Ralph opened his mouth, "You should only play with other children who are nice, like you. What was the next bad choice?"

"I shouldn't have crossed the railroad tracks?"

"Yes, exactly," said Dad. "Rules are made to keep us safe. Once you go across those railroad tracks," he added, "You are out of sight of the house. And that's a big part of the reason we made that rule."

"Bad choices lead to bad decisions," concluded Dad. "Just like good choices lead to good decisions. The next time you have to make a decision - like whether or not you are going to do something or go somewhere - you should first think about whether that action or choice is good or bad. If it could lead you to trouble, it's almost always a bad choice."

Dad had one more question. "Did you even tell Ayesha where you were going? She didn't seem to know where you were."

"I told her, but she was on her phone. I don't know if she heard me."

"Ah," said Dad. He frowned. "I guess we need to find another babysitter." He pushed his chair out from the table and stood up. "It sounds like hiring Ayesha to babysit you may have been a bad choice on the part of your mother and I."

Ralph went and laid down on the couch for a few minutes. Noodle came and licked the tears from his cheeks. He rested his chin on Ralph's arm, as if to say, "I'm here!"

Mom came home, and Dad told her everything that had happened that day. Mom didn't say much - she just looked at him in a sympathetic way. That evening, she made Ralph's favorite dinner - spaghetti and garlic toast.

When it was time to get ready for bed, Ralph took a bath and brushed his teeth. He got into bed. As he lay there sleepily, Noodle hopped up on the bed and shifted to his usual spot near the bottom, right next to Ralph's leg. Mom came in to say goodnight, as she almost always did. "Why did you do it, Ralph?" she asked.

"Why did I go across the railroad tracks with Johnny?" Mom nodded.

"He's one of the cool kids at school, Mom! I just wanted to be cool. And he's got really awesome shoes," Ralph added. He knew it didn't make sense, but that's how he felt.

Mom shook her head. "Having nice shoes does not make a person a good friend. I don't want to see you anywhere near that boy again! Someone like that will get into trouble and take you with them every time," she said.

"Besides, Ralph," she added, "you'll always be cool to me, no matter who your friends are." She stroked his hair.

Ralph nodded. "I won't go near him again, Mom. And I won't cross the railroad tracks either." He thought how good it felt to be home, safe in his own bed.

Mom smiled and kissed his forehead. "I love you, Ralph," she said. "Good night! And good night, Noodle!" she added as an afterthought, turning the light off as she left the room.

"Yip! Yip!" said Noodle.

Chapter4: The Lemonade Stand

Emily woke up to sunlight streaming through her window. She was tired, so she had slept late this morning. Her mom came in to help her dress, then lifted Emily into her wheelchair.

"Emily, you really need a new wheelchair!" Mom looked sad. "This old thing is getting rusty. I wish we had the money to buy it for you." Emily nodded. Her wheelchair sometimes squeaked when she rolled it, and the left wheel sometimes stuck. Also, the seat was dirty. She'd had the wheelchair for four years. It *would* be nice to have one that worked properly and didn't make so much noise.

While Emily was eating breakfast, Ralph showed up. "Sam is coming home today!" he announced happily. His best friend had been on vacation for the first few weeks of summer, but today was the day he would finally be home!

Emily was a little sad. She hoped Ralph wouldn't forget about her when his friend returned! They had been playing together almost every day since they had met. Sometimes Ralph came to her house, and they played games or cards. Other days, she made the short trip down to Ralph's house where they often built things with Legos, or sometimes even watched a cartoon on TV.

"Let's watch a video," suggested Ralph.

Emily rolled her wheelchair into the living room. She heard the squeak of the chair as she maneuvered around the couch. "I need a new wheelchair, but my family can't afford one," she explained to Ralph as she pulled up the brake to keep her chair in place.

Ralph looked interested. "How much do they cost?"

Emily considered. She had heard her parents talking about this very thing about a month ago. "About

$1,000," she sighed. It seemed like an enormous amount of money to her!

Ralph looked wistful. "I wish I could help buy you one! But I'm not really old enough to get a job. If I was a grown-up, I would give you the money myself!" he said grandly.

Emily smiled at him. "Thanks, Ralph!" He really was a good friend, she thought.

After lunch, Emily was still tired. "Why don't you take a nap, Emily!" Mom said worriedly. So, Ralph went home, but he was still thinking about Emily's wheelchair. It was the first thing he mentioned to his mother when he arrived at his house.

"Can't we do something to help her, Mom?" he asked worriedly. "Emily deserves a good wheelchair. She's such a nice person."

Mom smiled her gentle smile at him. "That's very sweet of you to want to help, Ralph!" she said fondly. Her face, though, clouded over a little. "But we really don't have that kind of money right now to give away. We also have many bills we have to pay," she explained to him.

"Maybe we could come up with the money somehow," mused Ralph. He remembered a story he had seen on TV about a boy - who was about Ralph's age - who'd raised money to purchase food for poor people. If that boy was able to collect money to help other people, he thought, why couldn't I?

Suddenly, there was a knock on the door. Ralph looked out the window. Sam was back! "Sam!" he howled, flinging open the door!

Ralph grinned at his best friend. They slapped hands. "How was California?" he asked his friend.

Sam grinned. "Very sunny." Unconsciously, he ran a hand through his curly hair, which was usually brown, but was now almost blonde from being in the California sunshine for two weeks.

"Lucky!" said Ralph enviously. "We never get to go anywhere! Well, 'cept sometimes to see Aunt Minnie," he added. Aunt Minnie was his mother's older, unmarried sister who lived in upstate New York. It didn't really count as a vacation, though, because Aunt Minnie only lived an hour away. And Ralph never looked forward to those visits the way he would look forward to a fun vacation. Aunt Minnie liked her cats well enough, but she wasn't too happy to have a young boy running through her house. Ralph tried to get out of those visits whenever he could.

"What did you do in California?" Ralph asked curiously.

"We mainly went to the beach," Sam responded. "It was really hot there! And we went and saw a big gold bridge, and we went to some theme parks."

"You saw the Golden Gate Bridge?" chimed in Ralph's mother, overhearing their conversation as she walked through the room. "I haven't been to San Francisco in years. It's beautiful out there!" Ralph remembered his mother had lived in San Francisco for a time as a little girl. Sometimes, she told him stories of when she used to go to Chinatown with her brothers and sisters to get Chinese food.

Just then, Noodle came into the kitchen, wanting to play. "Arf!" he barked loudly, his brown eyes snapping as he ran in circles, carrying his bone in his mouth.

"You got a dog?" cried Sam jealously.

Ralph smiled proudly. "This is Noodle! I got him at the beginning of the summer," he added. "This is my best friend Sam," Ralph told Noodle. The dog ran around Sam a few times, then stopped and looked up at the new boy with friendly eyes. "Yip! Yip!" he said.

"That's his way of saying 'hello!' Ralph told Sam. "And, hey, Sam... There's a new girl down the street! She's really nice. Her name is Emily, and she's in a wheelchair," he told his friend.

Sam frowned. "A wheelchair? What's wrong with her?" he asked curiously.

Ralph thought hard. "I think she said she was in a car accident?" Emily had told him, but it was a few weeks ago, back when they first met. So, he didn't quite remember. "She has a dog too! It's a little one named Ruby. She barks a lot... like Noodle does," he grinned.

"What do you want to do?" asked Sam. "Do you want to play Legos? Or go on the internet and play video games? Or...?" asked Sam. He continued to name different activities they could do together.

Ralph was thinking, though. "Sam... there's one thing about Emily, though... she needs a new wheelchair."

Sam looked puzzled. "So?"

"Maybe we could help her to get one!" said Ralph.

"How?" wondered Sam. "That would probably be a lot of money, right? To buy a wheelchair?"

"She said it would be like $1,000," answered Ralph. Sam whistled, impressed. "That's a lot of money!"

"I'm going to ask Mom for ideas how we could come up with it," said Ralph. "There must be something we can do to help!"

Mom was cleaning out one of the upstairs closets when Ralph found her. He asked her his question.

Mom blinked. "Well, sometimes kids sell things, or put up a lemonade stand when they want to raise money," she told him. "I'm not sure you could raise $1,000 that way, but you can try!"

"Can we do it tomorrow?" Ralph asked.

"Sure!" Mom smiled. "I can email the ladies in my book club and call some friends. I'm sure that when people hear why you're having the lemonade stand, they will be happy to contribute!"

Ralph and Sam walked down to Mr. Miller's Art Store to get markers and poster board to make a sign. Mom had given them enough money to buy two pieces of poster board.

When they got home, they sat down and wrote, "RALPH AND SAM'S LEMONADE STAND! $2" - on one piece of poster board. They weren't sure, though, what they should write on the other piece of poster board. Should they make two signs?

Mom came over to admire their work. "Looks good, boys! On the other one, though, why don't you write that the money raised will be used to buy your friend a wheelchair? People will be even more likely to help if they know it's for a good cause." So, on the other sign, Sam wrote, "To help our friend Emily buy a wheelchair!"

When dad came home that evening, he was very happy with both the idea and Ralph's motivation for doing it. "That's my boy!" Dad said, tousling Ralph's hair. He and Mom looked at Ralph proudly. "Maybe I'll run to the store and get some extra lemonade mix tonight! It sounds like you might be needing it tomorrow," he pointed out to Ralph. "And some plastic cups might help, too!" he added.

"I can't wait to tell Emily about what we're doing!" said Ralph happily.

"Good idea!" said Mom. "In fact, let's run down to her house right now! "

Ralph was so excited, he could barely sleep that night! Also, he was worried. What if it rained the next day? Luckily, the next day dawned clear and beautiful.

Right after Ralph had walked and fed Noodle, Sam arrived at his house. The boys set up the old table Mom had dragged out of the basement for them to use. They taped up the signs on the house behind them - and waited.

Their first customers were Emily and her Mom. Emily was so happy, Ralph thought she looked as though she was glowing. Her Mom looked happy, but in a different way. She looked as though she was about to cry.

Emily *was* happy. She had been afraid Ralph wouldn't want to be friends with her anymore since his best friend had come back. But not only did he still want to be friends, but he and his other friend were even doing something nice for her! She felt very relieved. And excited that she might finally be able to get a new wheelchair, she thought!

Ralph and Sam's neighbor from down the street, Mrs. Smith, walked by with her cat. "Lemonade? How nice!" she said excitedly in her shrill voice. "Let me run home and get some money." A few minutes later, she came back with 4 dollars in quarters, and took two cups of lemonade. Then she looked at Ralph with her bright, alert eyes, and slipped him an envelope as she walked off down the street talking to her cat.

Ralph opened the envelope and gawked. There were five twenty-dollar bills inside! "She just gave us one hundred dollars!"

When Mom came outside, though, she was not surprised. "I told you people like to support a good cause! And I think you can expect some more visitors soon," she added mysteriously. Ralph was puzzled. What did she mean by that?

A few minutes later, seven elderly ladies came walking down the street. "You must be Ralphie!" one said to him, pinching his cheek. "Your mother is in my book club! She talks about you all the time."

Ralph tried his best not to scowl. He didn't like having his cheek pinched, and he didn't like being called Ralphie either. However, when the lady gave him five dollars for a cup of lemonade, he was somewhat reconciled. Every one of the ladies bought a cup of lemonade, and each one gave them a whole five dollars for their cup! Then they stopped inside to visit his mom for a few minutes.

Word began to spread around the neighborhood about the lemonade stand and the reason for it. People walking down the street stopped to ask about it. Mom bought Noodle out to them, tying his leash to the table leg. "People love dogs!" she smiled. "Maybe he will bring you some more business."

Dad came home at 11 o'clock. He helped them to count their money. "So far, you have three hundred four dollars!" he said, looking impressed. He looked at the short line that had backed up. "Maybe I'll run to the store to get a bit more lemonade mix... Just in case!"

After he had left, and after they waited on the last few customers, it got quiet. Ralph was happy they had raised so much; still, though, he was a little disappointed. They were a long way from a thousand dollars, he thought.

When Dad returned, he noticed Ralph's crestfallen face. "Don't give up, Ralph!" he said encouragingly. "Don't be upset! You have raised a lot of money so far! You can do this … no question about it! If you have to, maybe you can set up the stand for another day or two. Three hundred and four dollars is not bad at all, and the day is not even over yet!"

Suddenly, a van pulled up. The writing on the side of the van said, "Channel 13… We have the news that matters!"

Sam gawked at it. "I wonder what this is about?"

Two men got out. One of them, Ralph thought, was rather … *oily* looking. Ralph couldn't think of any other word to describe him. He was wearing a suit. The other man just looked like a normal person. He had blonde hair.

"I'm Al from Channel 13," said the man in the suit smoothly. "We have our offices at the other end of Carberry Street."

"Oh, yeah," said Ralph. "I think maybe I walked past them once or twice."

The man smiled. "We like the human-interest angle of this," he went on. "It's nice to see kids doing something to help a friend in need."

Ralph was confused by the first part of the man's sentence, but the second part sounded nice. "We just feel bad because she needs a new wheelchair, but her family can't afford it," he explained.

"Would you like to be on television?" asked the normal man. "We'd like to do a story about this. Cute dog, by the way," he added, smiling down at Noodle.

"Woof!" replied Noodle, wagging his tail. The man laughed aloud.

"He can talk back!" said the oily man. "I have dachshunds, too!" he told Ralph, opening his wallet to show the boys a picture of his dogs. Ralph decided the man was OK, after all. Anyway, he had cute dogs.

"Put him on camera for the story!" said the normal man. "People love dogs!"

"That's what my mom said, too!" said Ralph.

"My name is Jake, by the way!" said the blonde-haired man.

"And I'm Al." The oily man introduced himself again. He pulled a microphone out of the truck and began to fix his hair as Jake set up the camera.

"We're here on Carberry Street where two boys are working hard today to help their friend..." began the news anchor, as Jake filmed.

Ralph and Sam got to talk on camera! When they were finished, Jake asked for their phone numbers. "We may be able to help you out," he said, very nicely, Ralph thought. He liked the blonde man.

The next day, the news station called. When they had aired the story, it was very popular with the viewers. Better yet, a wheelchair company had seen the news story and called the station. They wanted to donate a free wheelchair for Emily!

Ralph's dad said he was proud of the town for coming together to help get Emily a new wheelchair. He was proudest of all, though, of Ralph. "You took the initiative to make it happen, Ralph!" he said.

"What's initiative mean, Dad?" asked Ralph.

Dad explained with a smile. "It means being the first, son. You were the first to help Emily and, because of you, other people began to help too."

"What should we do with the money we raised?" Ralph wondered. They hadn't had to spend any of it on the wheelchair, after all.

Dad thought for a moment. "Let's go ahead and give it to Emily's family. Her Dad said they haven't had much money lately because she has so many medical bills. Maybe it will help the family to buy food."

One day, Emily's new wheelchair arrived. Ralph and Sam went down to see it. It was much nicer than her old one, Ralph thought.

Ralph thought Emily looked especially pretty sitting in her new chair. She had her long, blonde hair up in a pink bow that day, and she was holding her little dog, Ruby, on her lap. Ruby growled at the boys, but because Emily liked the boys, Ruby tolerated them. Ruby adored Emily.

Sam grinned at him. "This is awesome, Ralph! We did good!"

Emily's Mom smiled at them through happy tears, and said, "I'm so glad we moved to Carberry Street. Ralph, you are the best friend Emily has ever had!"

And Emily gave Ralph her thanks with a hug.

Chapter 5: The New Baby

July had arrived on Carberry Street. It was the hottest time of the year in the city - so hot that most people stayed inside, in the air-conditioning, avoiding the sticky, stifling heat. But Ralph almost never stayed inside in the summer. Besides, he was happy now because almost all his friends had finally returned from their summer vacations! Only his next-door neighbor, Dylan, was still away. But Dylan was staying with his cousin in Chicago for almost the whole summer, so he would not arrive back in the neighborhood until it was almost time for school to start back up. Anyway, Ralph was *glad* to be playing outside again with his friends - in fact, he was happier than he had been for a long time! The heat never bothered the boys from the Carberry Street neighborhood. They were usually having too much fun even to notice it!

"Hmmm... What should we do today?" thought Ralph to himself. He might go and get his best friend Sam, and they could play a game of baseball in the big field on the corner. Maybe they could bring some of the other kids to join them, too! Or perhaps he could gather some of the neighborhood kids and they could all take Noodle for a walk around the block. Or maybe they could even go to the park and look for new bugs! Knowing how much he liked to look for insects, Ralph's father had gotten him a new bug-catching kit at the store a few nights before. The children had already used it several times. They had gone to the park one evening and found two crickets, an interesting, colorful worm, and even a few lightning bugs! Ralph loved to look at lightning bugs. He had actually kept them overnight, then let them go in the park again the next morning.

On a beautiful summer morning such as this one, Ralph thought, the possibilities of things to do seemed endless! Now that his friends were back in the neighborhood, each new summer's day was like a giant blank canvas, just waiting to be filled with friends and fun escapades.

However, Ralph's life was about to change. He would soon find out just how much once he made the short trip down the stairs of the family's townhouse.

This Ralph did, hurtling himself down the stairs with Noodle tagging along at his heels. The dog never left Ralph's side. Wherever Ralph went, his short little legs followed. When Ralph left the house, Mom told him, Noodle would sit near the door and wait for him to return. "Such a loyal little dog!" Dad had said affectionately one day, stroking Noodle's head. "That's your boy, Ralph!"

Mom and Dad were sitting at the kitchen table having coffee. The first alarm bells went off in Ralph's head. Why was Dad home? Today was a weekday. Dad should have gone to work a long time ago. "Dad, shouldn't you be at work?" Ralph asked curiously.

Dad smiled ... no, *beamed* at Ralph. In fact, Dad was smiling from ear to ear. Suspiciously, Ralph glanced over at Mom. Her face was also wreathed in smiles.

Mom looked, well, *proud*, almost! Ralph frowned. Somehow, he had a bad feeling about this.

"Sit down, Ralph," said Dad.

Ralph looked at him, askance. He wondered if he were in trouble for something. But no, if that were true, his parents would not look so happy. Ralph sat - and waited for someone to tell him what was going on.

"I went to the doctor with your mother this morning, Ralph. That's why I'm home," said Dad. Now, he had a very serious look on his face.

"We're going to have a baby, Ralph!" Mom burst out. Tears began to run down her face. They were tears of happiness, though, because she was smiling at the same time. "We've been trying, I mean... well, ummm..." she looked at Dad and smiled.

Ralph considered. "But you already have a baby. Me!"

Mom laughed as though Ralph had said something funny. He hadn't been kidding, though.

Mom reached around the table and put her arm around him. "And you always will be my baby, Ralph! My first baby!" she told him. "This baby could never take your place. There will just be two babies in our family. I have enough love for two of you," she told him earnestly, her blue eyes looking into Ralph's green ones.

Ralph considered. He had seen little babies at the store. Also, Sam had a baby sister. Babies were OK, Ralph supposed. But they sure made a lot of noise! And sometimes they even smelled. Ralph wrinkled his nose at the thought. He wasn't sure if he wanted a baby or not, and he told his parents so. "I'll tell you what," he said, "let me go to Sam's and spend some time with him and his baby sister! And when I come back tonight, I will let you know if I want a baby or not." He left the house, leaving his parents staring after him.

Sam only lived a few houses away. Sam's mother opened the door. Ralph thought Sam's mother was nice. She was very different than his own mother, of course, but he liked her anyway. Mrs. Gianetti was full of energy, friendly, and blonde, while Ralph's mother was gentle, quiet, and had brown hair. But Sam wouldn't trade her for anything in the world. Even though, he added grudgingly to himself, she was having a baby.

"Hello, Ralph!" trilled Mrs. Gianetti happily. "It's good to see you! Sam really missed you on vacation, didn't you, Sam?" she asked, as he came into the room. "maybe another time you can come with us to California! I'm sure you'd love it there, and Sam would love to have you along!"

"That would be awesome!" Ralph told her excitedly. Maybe he would get a vacation someday, he thought, after all. She smiled at him again and went to the kitchen. But then, Ralph remembered why he had come in the first place.

"I'm not here to play today. I'm here on business," Ralph told Sam, using a phrase he sometimes heard his dad say. Sam looked puzzled. He scratched his face - an unconscious thing he sometimes did when he couldn't figure out what someone was talking about - and said, "What!?"

"It means I came to see your baby sister," Ralph explained.

"Oh!" Sam's face cleared again, but then he again grew puzzled when he thought about what Ralph had said. "Zara? Why?"

"My mom's going to have a baby," Ralph explained. "And so, I want to see yours so I can decide if I want one or not. Then I will go home and let my parents know." Ralph heard Sam's mom laughing from the kitchen, but he wasn't sure what she was laughing about. Maybe she was on the phone, he thought.

A few seconds later, she came out, but she was acting normally again. She had her usual smile. "That's wonderful, Ralph! Congratulations on becoming a big brother!"

Ralph hadn't quite thought of it that way, but he said "Thanks!" anyway.

"I will have to call your parents to congratulate them as well!" Mrs. Gianetti went on. She changed the subject. "Zara is taking a nap - she woke up very early this morning!" she exclaimed. "But she has been sleeping for a few hours, so let me wake her! Maybe we can all take her outside for a few minutes. It's going to be too hot for her to stay out there very long today," she added. "It's supposed to get up to 90 degrees today out there... Looks like another scorcher!"

Mrs. Gianetti went to get the baby. She returned with a sleepy-looking, pink and white, tiny... *human being* in her hands. It was funny, Ralph thought, but he hadn't paid that much attention to the baby before. Now that his family might have one, he was really interested. "How old is she again?" he asked.

"She's one year old," Sam told him.

Ralph reached out a hand to touch her. She wrapped her tiny fingers around one of his bigger one and looked at him with her big blue eyes. The first thing he thought was that she was actually very cute. And she didn't even smell very bad right now, either! He said this to Sam's mom, who laughed out loud. He got the feeling she was very amused by this whole thing.

Mrs. Gianetti went to get a blanket for them to sit on, and they all went outside. Most of the people on their street had what Ralph's dad called "city backyards"; A patch of grass surrounded by a tall fence. However, Mr. Gianetti worked in landscaping, which meant that he worked with trees and plants all day. Therefore, Sam's backyard looked like a small jungle! There were wood trellises with plants climbing up them. There were many bushes and trees. The boys found it was a fun place to play hide-and-seek.

Sam's mother spread the blanket out, and they all sat down on it. Mrs. Gianetti brought a book outside so they could read to the baby. Ralph decided that the baby was cute! Zara helped Mrs. Giannetti turn the pages in the book. The baby cooed and laughed a lot, and sometimes even chortled at the pictures in the book.

Suddenly, Mrs. Gianetti's cell phone rang, and she picked it up. It sounded, Ralph thought, like it was a friend of hers. They began to talk about a church event. "I'm not sure when the practice is!" she said to her friend. "Let me go inside and find out, Ok?" She mouthed to Sam, "Watch the baby," as she hurried into the house.

"Your mom lets you watch the baby?" Ralph asked, impressed.

"Only when she goes away for just a minute. Not for very long," Sam answered.

Zara sat and played with them for a few minutes. Suddenly, her unfocused eyes zeroed in on Ralph. She giggled and reached out her arms to him. Ralph's heart melted! He decided that having a baby might not be so bad after all. He hoped he got a little sister, he decided.

Suddenly, he saw a really cool bug on a leaf on one of the bushes! "Check this out, Sam!" he hollered, leaping for the bug. Ralph tended to get really excited when he saw new bugs. "I've never seen one like this before! Have you? "

Sam crawled over to look at the bug in his friend's hand. He commented on the markings. The little spots and stripes on the bug were very brightly colored.

"We should go look it up on the internet!" said Ralph. Sam responded, "Yes! As soon as we finish watching the ba..." his voice broke off. Ralph looked at his friend. Sam had turned around to look at the blanket. He was staring. Ralph turned around and stared too. The baby was gone!

Ralph would swear that his heart stopped at that moment. He looked at the door to the house. The sliding glass door was closed now. Had it been closed before? He couldn't remember. The boys walked around the yard. They peeked behind every tree and looked under every bush. There was no baby.

Sam took off for the house. Ralph had never seen anyone run so fast in his life. His friend pushed open the sliding glass door. "Mom! The baby!!! She's gone!"

The boys raced in the house. Mrs. Gianetti came around the corner, still on the phone. In her arms she held Zara.

It was as though the world, which Ralph felt had stopped for a minute, started to move again. Sam let out a huge sigh of relief. Mrs Gianetti, however, looked very stern. Her usual smile was gone from her face as she looked at the boys. "I will see you tomorrow," she said to her friend as she hung up the phone.

"I came outside and you were not paying any attention to the baby at all! You were so busy looking at that bug - or whatever it was - that you didn't even notice me come out and take her. You didn't even hear me shut the door. You can *not* leave a baby alone like that! Just in that minute, something very bad could happen. It only takes a second for a baby to... put the wrong thing in their mouth and choke, for example. All kinds of bad things can happen if you don't watch a baby carefully."
When Sam started to respond, she told him "Zara had picked up a rock and put it into her mouth. If I hadn't seen her, she might have tried to swallow it."

All of a sudden, it hit Ralph what a big *responsibility* having a baby was. But he was also jealous of Sam for having that responsibility. He decided that he definitely did want a baby brother or sister, after all. He liked Zara, but she was the Gianetti's baby. The baby his mother had would be *his* family's baby! When it was time to go home, he would have to leave this baby with Sam's family. But soon, his family would have a baby of their own.

He voiced his thoughts to Sam's mother. "Having a baby is a big responsibility, isn't it?"

Sam's mother was firm with the boys. "Having a baby to watch is a huge responsibility! And you should never be distracted from your responsibilities like you were today, Ralph. You and Sam should always stay mindful when you have a job to do, whether that job is something important like watching the baby, or something not quite as important, like taking out the trash or making your bed. People are counting on you to live up to your responsibilities," she said.

"I hope you boys have learned a lesson today!" Mrs. Gianetti added. Ralph thought that it was the first time that he had ever seen Sam's mom angry. She was usually cheerful.

Ralph took his leave of the family. Before he left, though, he gave Zara a little kiss on the cheek. He was extremely relieved that nothing bad had happened to her, and he was a little ashamed of his behavior. He was very sorry that he had been distracted by the bug.

That night, when Ralph was in bed, his mother came to say good night to him, as she always did.

"I decided I do want the baby, Mom, so you can go ahead and take it," announced Ralph. His mom went off into gales of laughter. Ralph wondered why everyone was laughing at him today. It was getting really annoying!

Mom tried to explain. "Ralph, having a baby is not like getting a dog, where you can decide whether or not you want to get one. There is already a baby growing in my tummy, and it is going to come whether or not you decide you want it."

Ralph considered. He guessed he had known that babies come from tummies - he had seen pregnant women many times - but he had just never really thought about it very much.

"A few months from now, Ralph, you will be able to feel my tummy and feel the baby kick," his mom tried to explain. "You will get to watch the baby grow in my tummy, and you'll get to see it right away when it is born!"

"And it will be my baby, too!" said Ralph fiercely. He thought of Sam's cute little blue-eyed baby sister. "And I will always watch the baby carefully," he added, thinking about what had happened today at Sam's house.

Ralph's mom smiled her sweet smile. "Yes, Ralph! It will be your baby too. "And yes, you can watch it very carefully," she added. She flipped off the light so he could go to sleep.

But Ralph had one more question. "Will it be Noodle's baby, too?"

Because light streamed in from the hallway, Ralph was able to see Noodle's head pop up at the sound of his name. "Arf!" said Noodle. Then he made a strange little strangled sound that sounded a bit like "Yes."

Mom laughed. "Yes! The baby will belong to the whole family. Even Noodle."

"Goodnight, Mom!" said Ralph. He turned over and went to sleep.

Chapter 6: A Day at the Pool

Sam woke up early on that Saturday morning. He wasn't sure exactly why. Perhaps it was because he had gone to sleep early the night before. His family had gone to a baseball game yesterday, and he had been tired when they returned. But now he was awake and he couldn't go back to sleep. It was really early! he thought. His parents weren't awake yet. Even his baby sister was still asleep.

He walked downstairs and got a bowl of his favorite cereal, Lucky Charms. How glad he was that Mom had remembered to buy it at the store this week! Last week, he'd had to eat oatmeal for breakfast for the whole week! He didn't like oatmeal much.

Sam had just settled down to watch cartoons on TV when he heard the baby crying. After that, the house started to come to life. His mom's tones wafted down the stairs as she sang to the baby. She always sang to Zara as she changed her diaper and dressed her in the morning. Sam's mom was kind of loud, but he didn't mind. Most of the time, he actually liked it. Sam's dad was really quiet, though.

Dad came down the stairs a few minutes later. "You're up early, Sam! Want me to make you some breakfast? Did you already eat your Lucky Charms?"

Sam grinned. His dad knew him well! "Yeah, Dad, I did," he replied.

"I was thinking maybe we'd go to the pool today," Dad went on.

Sam was instantly excited. The pool! They hadn't been to the pool in ages. "Yeah!" he shouted and ran to put on his bathing suit.

When he came back downstairs, Dad smiled at him. "Calm down, son! We're not leaving quite yet."

Mom came down the stairs next, baby in hand. She set about feeding the baby as she and Dad talked about the family's plans for the day.

Finally, it was time to go. The family piled into their van and headed off down the street to the neighborhood pool.

When they arrived at the pool, Sam saw two boys from school. They weren't his best friends, he thought, but sometimes he hung around with them when he had nothing better to do. Their names were Tim and Christian. He didn't know them very well, but they seemed OK. They saw him right away. "Sam!!!" they shouted. The three boys ran off together.

Sam stared at the sparkling blue water and couldn't wait to get into the pool! He'd been coming to this pool since he was under three years old, so he knew exactly where everything was, and what the most fun things to do were here.

Sam saw his parents walk by and carry Zara through the gate of the splash playground. The splash playground was for babies and toddlers, and it was separated from the big pool by a chain-link fence and gate.

"Altogether now!" shouted Christian, and the boys lined up and prepared to jump into the pool together. "One... two... three!!!!" shouted Tim, and they all ran and jumped into the pool at the same time, drenching everyone around them with water, including a sweet-looking elderly couple, as well as some teenage girls who were in the pool. Sam noticed this immediately and apologized to everyone. Sam's friends, however, either didn't notice - or didn't care. They continued to behave in a boisterous way, splashing and yelling, not showing respect for anyone else in the pool. The teenage girls glared at the boys and moved to the other side of the pool. The elderly couple pretended to ignore the boys, but Sam noticed that they moved further down the side of the pool towards the deep end, away from the boys.

Sam had always been told that he was very mature for his age, and when he hung around with boys like this, he found it easy to believe it was true. He was totally uninterested in being around this kind of behavior. He began to sort of edge away from the boys, trying to find a way to make an exit and leave them. He knew his parents wouldn't like him being around these boys, either.

Sam looked down in the direction of the snack bar. He must be getting hungry again already, he thought, because the smell of the food was making his stomach water. It was then that he saw Emily. He didn't even recognize her at first without her wheelchair. She was sitting in a white pool chair. Sam noticed that someone was lying in a long chair next to her - maybe her mother? From this far away, Sam couldn't tell. Besides, he had only met her mother one time, so he hardly remembered what she looked like.

Sam decided to go over and say hi. After all, by this time, he was extremely bored with his friends' rude behavior anyway. Really, Emily was more Ralph's friend than his, but anyway, he thought she was nice.

Emily didn't see him when he approached her. He thought she looked a bit sad, though. "Hey, Emily!" He said. She brightened up when she recognized him. "Hi Sam!" He thought she looked extremely happy to see him. Her Mom was asleep next to her, so maybe she wanted somebody to hang out with, he thought. For some reason, Sam felt sorry for her. He wondered what it was like to have to stay in a wheelchair all the time. He wanted to ask her, but he knew that would not be polite, so he just sat and waited for her to say something.

Emily was looking longingly at the kids laughing and splashing in the pool. She probably wanted to go in, he thought. So he said, "Are you wanting to go into the pool? I bet your mom will take you in when she wakes up."

Emily said, "I was just missing how I used to be able to go into the pool by myself."

"Oh," said Sam. He wasn't sure exactly what to say, but he felt bad for her. She talked on about it for a few minutes, and so he just stayed quiet and listened. Maybe it would help her just to have someone to listen, he thought. He wished he could make her smile. She looked so much better when she smiled, he thought.

Suddenly, he heard shouting behind him. "SAMson!" hollered Christian's voice. He looked over to see Christian and Tim hanging off the side of the pool, hooting at him. They looked unhappy. Sam thought maybe they were mad because he had gone off and left them. "What do you want to hang out with *HER* for?" Tim looked with distaste at the wheelchair under the table, then gave Emily the same look. "Why are you over here talking to a girl!?" Christian asked. Both boys were oblivious to all of the dirty looks they were getting from other people in the pool. Again, Sam wondered if they didn't notice the looks, or if they just didn't *care*.

"Why don't you two go away?" asked Sam crossly. Honestly, he was trying to be nice, but they were really getting on his nerves. He wished they would just go somewhere else and leave him - and especially Emily - alone. He didn't like the mean way they were looking at her.

"Are you going to kiss your girlfriend?" Christian asked, while Tim erupted into a chorus of "Ooooooh's!" Sam stood up, furious! He was ready to hit the other boy. Luckily, he didn't have to.

"What exactly is going on here!?" Emily's mom had woken up, and she was not happy. She was glaring at the boys. For a moment, she reminded Sam of a protective mother tigress he had seen in a cartoon, and despite all the tension around him, he almost grinned at the thought. Whenever he saw her before, he thought, she had been kind of quiet. She was not like that now.

Her glance moved over to Sam for a moment. She seemed to realize that he was not the problem. Perhaps she remembered that he was Ralph's best friend, because she gave a little smile and nodded at him. Then her angry expression returned, and it was directed back to Tim and Christian, who were looking alarmed.

"Where are your parents!?" Emily's mom asked the boys.

Both of them started a little. "They're not here," mumbled Christian. Sam noticed he was now looking a little shamefaced.

"Oh." Emily's mom had a look on her face as though everything were clear to her now. "well, if you don't go away and leave my kid alone, I will be finding out their phone numbers and giving them a call! "

With a few backwards glares at Sam, the boys moved away. For the first time, Sam looked at Emily. She looked totally humiliated. She had already been sad before this incident, so now she looked even worse. Sam tried to rack his brain for something nice he could do for her.

"Be right back. I have to go to the bathroom!" he told Emily and her mother. Her mother smiled at him. "Did I hear you standing up to those boys?"

Sam's answer was direct. "Yes. They've been acting really rude all day! And I was just tired of it. At school sometimes, they are nice. So, I don't know what's wrong with them today."

Emily's mom shrugged. She frowned. "Yes, sometimes when boys are away from their parents, they act like that."

"Well, my mom always says I shouldn't get into fights," Sam told her. "So, I'm glad you woke up, 'cause I was getting really mad!"

Emily's mom had one more question. "Aren't you the boy who did the lemonade stand with Sam?"

Emily spoke for the first time. "Yes, Mom. Sam is Ralph's best friend."

Emily's mom wiped something out of her eyes. Was it a tear? Sam wondered. Maybe she just had something in her eye. But when she spoke, her voice sounded a little bit misty. "Well, Sam, you've been a great friend to our family, then. I've never seen Emily so happy as she has been since we moved to this neighborhood.

Sam smiled at her. "I have to go to the bathroom, ma'am," he said again. It was a half-truth, but they did not have to know that yet.

Sam went to the bathroom, but then he headed over to the splash pool to find his parents. He went through the gate and passed tons of screaming, splashing kids who were climbing in and playing around the colorful water playground. He looked for his mother's pink bathing suit and found her on the other side of the pool. His dad appeared to be sleeping in a pool lounge chair, while his mother and Zara were playing at the very edge of the pool. Zara had the blue bucket they had bought for her to play with. Ralph watched as the baby filled it with water, then dumped it out, crowing and clapping after each time, as though it were the funniest thing in the world. He grinned. His baby sister was really cute sometimes!

Then he remembered why he had come. "Mom, can I have some money for ice-cream?" He gave his mom a quick rundown on what had happened. "...and I thought if I gave her an ice-cream, it might cheer her up."

As usual, his mom decided to give him a little lesson from what had occurred. He wanted to roll his eyes, but at least, he figured, this would be a good lesson, because he had done something nice this time. He was right.

His mother began, "Ok, Sam, I'm really proud of you. First of all, you went and spent time with someone that probably none of the other kids really wanted to spend time with, because she can't go in the pool. Secondly, you sort of stood up for her - and yourself - when the boys were teasing you both. You know I don't like you fighting, though," she added, as Sam opened his mouth. "I'm glad it didn't get to that! because there are ways of standing up for yourself without fighting. Anyway, now you're also doing a very nice thing to want to buy her ice - cream to cheer her up! Sam," his mother said, "I am very proud of you today. You really are a good kid!"

Sam blushed to the roots of his brown hair. He should be used to his mom by now, he thought, but praise still made him feel shy sometimes - even when it was only his mom giving it.

Sam's mom gave him twenty dollars! He stared at it in shock. She smiled at him. "There's another lesson, Sam. When you do good things, good things will come back to you! So maybe you can buy an ice-cream for both of you, and then you can buy that little LEGO set you've been eyeballing every time we go to the store." Sam laughed. He didn't even know his mother had noticed!

Sam went to the snack bar and bought two giant chocolate-covered ice-cream bars. He went back to where Emily was sitting and handed one to her.

Her face lit up. "I love ice-cream!!!!"

"It seems like girls mostly do," Sam said, and started to laugh.

"But boys like it too," Emily protested.

"*Everyone* likes ice-cream!" Emily's Mom chimed in. And they talked and bantered like that for a little bit longer. Then Sam's parents showed up with Zara.

"So nice to meet you. You must be Emily's mom!" bubbled Sam's mother. Emily's mom looked a little overwhelmed by her first. Sam had noticed that his mom had that effect on people sometimes, because she never stopped talking. But once you got used to her, though, she was really nice. Emily's mom seemed to figure that out, because she eventually began to smile and talk to Sam's parents. Sam's mom and Emily's mom made plans to meet one morning for coffee at the neighborhood coffee shop. Then, in a flurry of goodbyes, Sam's family left the pool.

Zara cried on the way home. Sam, who was sitting in the backseat with her, stroked her head. He figured maybe she was tired from the heat. Sometimes the crying got on his nerves, but he was used to it. He figured, when you have a baby in the house, it's something you have to get used to.

Sam was exhausted. Between the baseball game yesterday and the time at the pool today, he had been in the sun for the most part of two days. He decided to go to bed early again.

As he went to sleep, he thought again about the day at the pool. He was glad he had sat with Emily at the pool today and also bought her the ice cream. His last thought before he went to sleep was that he liked the feeling he got when he did nice things for people. It made them happy, but it made him feel happy too!

Chapter 7: The Game

The summer continued to roll by, and suddenly, it was August. And it was still hot... So hot! None of the other kids on Carberry Street minded the heat at all, thought Emily, but *she* did. The heat made her tired. She already got tired easily, but the heat made it even worse. It made her not want to go outside at all. The only thing that made the afternoons tolerable was the fact that it rained almost every afternoon in the summer. The rain tended to cool everything down a bit. Emily looked forward to those afternoons. Sometimes it was cool enough that her mom would even let her sit outside in her wheelchair. Then Emily could sit on the front step with Ruby on her lap and watch the city go by around her. There was always something new to look at on busy Carberry Street.

Emily was getting used to her new home in the city. It was much more exciting than living on a farm! At all hours of the day, Emily would see fire trucks and police cars go blaring by. Cars raced by, honking at each other in their eternal quests to get to wherever they were going - and quickly. And, when Mom put Emily outside, she might even talk to the people going by. The people on Carberry Street were very nice, she thought. Even Mrs. Smith, the woman that all the kids called, "the crazy old cat lady" - because she had 7 cats living with her - was friendly, if a bit strange. Emily wondered why Mrs. Smith's husband didn't live with her. Every now and then, they would see him come to the house and visit, but then leave. Maybe he didn't like cats, Emily thought to herself with a grin.

While she was sitting outside in the afternoons, Emily had also met some of the other children in the neighborhood. While only she, Ralph, and Sam lived on this block, there were more children across and down the street. There was a boy named Andy she had met one day when he walked past her on the way to Ralph's house. She had also seen twin girls who lived in the next block. Emily had only seen them from far away - they hadn't come down to her block yet, but Sam had told her about them. And there was an older girl named Patty who lived across and then down the street.

Emily had her mom, it was true, but it was different with a grown-up. Mom didn't really understand certain things. She couldn't always talk to her mother the way she could talk to other kids.

At least she had her little dog Ruby to keep her company, thought Emily. Ruby could always be found by Emily's side. She never wanted to go away from Emily even for a little bit. When Emily was in bed, Ruby could be found under the covers, sleeping up against her mistress's leg, or snuggled up next to her. The rest of the time, as Emily sat in her wheelchair, the white dog sat on her lap. When she woke up in the morning, Ruby would be sitting and waiting to attack her face with kisses. Her life would be much emptier without Ruby. Emily thought that both she and Ralph were very lucky in the pets they had chosen. And Ruby and Noodle even liked each other. Ruby usually didn't like other dogs very much -

but Noodle was such a friendly, happy dog that Ruby seemed to accept him.

Emily was thrilled one morning when Ralph and Sam showed up at the door to visit her. Her mom had just finished dressing her, and she was sitting at the table getting ready to eat a bowl of oatmeal with butter and heaps of brown sugar - Emily's favorite breakfast. Her dad had teased her and said her teeth would fall out because of all the sugar. Emily wasn't offended. She was used to her dad's constant teasing.

The children sat at the table and talked while Emily ate. "Let's play a board game," suggested Ralph when she was finished eating. Sam shrugged. "Sure! Let's play Monopoly!" He knew it was one of Ralph's favorite games.

When they played Monopoly, Ralph always wanted to be the banker. He liked to be in charge of the money. Emily noticed he always looked intense when they played any game and Ralph didn't like to lose. Once, she had even seen him cry when they were playing a video game and he lost.

They had only been playing for a few minutes when Emily saw Ralph quietly take money from the bank and slip it in with his own money. She gasped, surprised. "Ralph! You cheated!"

He burst into tears and pretended to look shocked. The first thing he said was, "No I did not!" Then... "Please don't tell my Dad!"

Emily was disappointed in Ralph's behavior. Seeing him watching her, she tried to rearrange her face so he couldn't tell how she felt. However, the disappointment must have shown on her face anyway, because Ralph began to cry even harder.

"Cheater! Let me be banker then!" Sam's sun-browned face was red, and his usually placid eyes were snapping at Ralph. Emily guessed that Sam didn't like it when people cheated.

Ralph howled, "I am not a cheater! I only took one ten-dollar bill!"

"Well, that makes you a cheater!" Sam shouted back.

"What on earth is going on here?" Emily looked over to see Mom standing at the door. She looked surprised by all of the noise.

"Ralph cheated, Mom," Emily said matter-of-factly. "I saw him stealing money from the bank."

Mom frowned. "Well, that was not a good thing to do, Ralph!" she said. "However, I still don't think that's a good reason for all of this noise!" she added.

"Sorry, Mom! We will keep it down now," said Emily, giving Sam a side glance. Sam, catching her look, said obediently, "Sorry, Mrs. Miller! I just got mad."

"It's ok, Sam," said Emily's Mom mildly, as she left the room.

After she left, though, Sam looked at Ralph. "I don't play games with cheaters!" he said sulkily. To Emily's surprise, Sam pushed back his chair and got up and left!

Emily felt sorry for Ralph. He was sitting there with tears streaming down his face. She wished there was something she could say to make him feel better. "It'll probably be alright," she told him softly. "He will just have to cool down so he's not so mad anymore." She reached over and touched Ralph's hand. "I'll still be your friend, Ralph," she said. And Emily knew that she always would. He had been her first real friend, and she would not abandon him. Ralph almost smiled. He looked slightly comforted by her kind words.

Their game was ruined by today's events, though, and Emily was sad when Ralph left a few minutes later, his eyes still filled with tears. "See you later, Ralph!" she said sympathetically, but he barely answered her. She felt sad because their day was ended and she wheeled herself to her bookshelf to get a book to read. Ruby, who had been sunning herself in a sunbeam from the window, came and jumped into her lap.

Meanwhile, at home, Ralph was very sad. Had he lost his best friend because of one mistake?

Ralph lay down on his bed and stared at the ceiling. Noodle seemed to sense his unhappiness. He jumped up onto the bed and snuggled against Ralph's shoulder, nestling his head into Ralph's shoulder.

When Ralph first arrived home, Mom was napping. After he had been there for a few minutes, though, she came into his room and saw his face. "What's the matter, Ralph?" she asked.

With his words punctuated by sobs, Ralph told his mother what had happened.

After listening to the story, his mother considered for a moment. "Ralph, you seem like you are mainly upset because Sam is mad at you."

"I am!" cried Ralph.

His mother looked unusually stern. "Ralph, you and Sam will make up, I'm sure. I'm more upset about the fact that you cheated. Cheating is just as bad as lying."

Ralph said, "I didn't think cheating was that big of a deal!"

Ralph's mom was emphatic. "It is, Ralph, because cheating gives you an unfair advantage! I don't blame Sam for being angry with you."

"What does that mean, Mom... unfair advantage?" asked Ralph.

His mom sighed. "Ralph, any time you play a game with other people, there is what we call 'a level playing field.' That means everyone has the same chance of winning the game, so that is fair. But if you cheat, you give yourself more of a chance of winning the game. And that's not fair to the other players."

Ralph thought about it for a moment. He understood what she was saying.

"And furthermore, Ralph," said his mother, "I know that you *do* know that cheating is wrong, because your father and I have taught you that it is wrong."

Ralph just listened. He was a little ashamed now. He could understand why Sam was upset. But now, he also understood why he had to go apologize to his friends.

There was one more thing, though. "Mom, please don't tell Dad!" Ralph couldn't stand it when Dad was disappointed in him.

"Of course, I'm going to tell Dad." His mother was firm. "And you are going to be punished for this, Ralph," Mom added. "When you make bad choices, there will always be consequences. You need to learn that! And you definitely made a bad choice today." She softened. "Now go apologize to your friends! You have time before dinner. We're not going to eat until Dad comes home, in about an hour or so." P

"There's one more thing, Ralph," she added. "I'm sure Sam is also disappointed that you would cheat. You've been friends for a long time, and his feelings were probably hurt. Try to put yourself in his shoes. Imagine if you were Sam, and your best friend cheated in a game. Wouldn't your feelings be hurt?"

Ralph was thoughtful. "Yes, I think so."

His mother smiled at him for the first time since he had told her what had happened. "Very good, Ralph! Do you have used empathy to try to understand how he feels. Empathy is what happens when you try to put yourself in someone else's shoes to understand what they are feeling." She patted his knee. "Now go on! Wash up first," she said, looking at his dirty and tear-stained face. "Then she hugged him.

Ralph headed next-door to Sam's house. Mrs. Giannatti open the door. "Hi, Ralph," she said in a rather quiet way. Usually she was much friendlier to him. He thought she must have heard what had happened, and that made him want to start crying again. He liked Sam's bubbly mother.

Then Sam came up behind her. "He looks as sad as I feel," thought Ralph. He was glad to see that his friend was not angry anymore.

"Let's go play Legos!" said Sam. And then Ralph knew that all would be forgiven.

He still had to apologize, though. So, he waited until they were on the floor playing, and he said, "I'm sorry, Sam. I never thought of my cheating as hurting anyone. I've actually done it before," he said, quite honestly. "I just thought of it as a way to win."

Sam looked at him. "Well, it was really unfair to me and Emily," he said.

"Plus, you don't want to be a cheater, Ralph. And you know you could get into big trouble if you cheated at school."

Ralph looked bothered. "I've never cheated at school!"

"Well, how would I know?" Sam asked. " if you would cheat at one place, how do I know you wouldn't cheat at another?"

"But it's OK, Ralph," he said, seeing the sadness on his friend's face. "I just don't want you to get into trouble. And we're still best friends." He held up his hand for a fist bump, and the boys laughed and hooted. After the stress of the day, thought Ralph, it felt good to laugh again.

Later, when the boys went back downstairs, Ralph thought Sam's mom looked happy to see that they were getting along now. She smiled at the boys. "Is everything OK now?" she asked.

Sam grinned at her. "Yeah, Mom, everything's fine," he said, smiling. "Me and Ralph talked about everything."

When he left Sam's house, Ralph went down to apologize to Emily. Then after that, he knew he had one more person he had to face - his father. The thought made him feel rather gloomy. Ralph knew he would be in trouble. He might even get grounded! He didn't even mind so much if his dad was angry, he thought. But he hated when his father was disappointed in him.

When Ralph entered the house, Noodle was ecstatic to see him! He did his little dance he always did when Ralph returned home... Mom called it the "happy dance." Mom was smiling gently at Ralph. She looked happy to see him. Dad, though, looked a little bit more subdued,

"Hey Ralph!" He looked like he had just come home from work because he was still in his work clothes. "We'll talk after dinner, son," he added, a bit roughly, Ralph thought.

Ralph's stomach clenched. He was already nervous, but now he guessed they were going to have to put it off a little bit longer. Ralph just wanted to get it over with. Again, he wondered if he were going to be grounded. There was a carnival setting up down the street, and mom had promised to take him this weekend. But he knew he wouldn't be allowed to go if he were grounded.

Mom had made Chinese food for dinner. Normally, Ralph loved Sweet and Sour Chicken. But tonight, everything tasted like cardboard to him. He noticed that Dad didn't look at him much during dinner.

After dinner, Dad got right to the point. "Have a seat, Ralph," he said, pointing to the couch. He himself sat down in the big overstuffed armchair across from the television. "Ralph," he began, "You made a mistake today. Do you understand why what you did was wrong?"

"Yes, Dad," said Ralph, ashamed.

"Well," said Dad, "I understand you've already talked to your mom about it, so I believe you. But I have to say, Ralph, I would expect better of you. "

Dad continued, "You are grounded until Saturday morning. Remember that mistakes have consequences, Ralph. And if I hear of anything like this happening again, the punishment will be far more severe."

Ralph breathed a little easier. It was Wednesday now! So, he was only grounded for two days. He could still go to the carnival!

"I know, Dad! I promise, I won't do it again!" said Ralph.

Dad looked at him and gave him a half-smile. "Alright, Ralph. It's time to get ready for bed."

Lying in bed that night, as he got ready to go to sleep, Ralph felt like the luckiest boy in the world. He remembered a line of poetry that his mom often read to him... "God's in his heaven, All's right with the world!"

That was how he felt tonight. He had a really cool mom and dad. He had a best friend who had forgiven him, and even had the most awesome dog in the world, he thought, feeling the warmth of Noodle snuggled up against his leg. And this weekend he had the carnival to look forward to...

Mom popped her head in the door to say good night. "Love you sweetie!"

"Love you too Mom," Ralph responded happily.

Chapter 8: The Storyteller

It almost the end of August. Ralph could not believe it was nearly time for school to start again! It had been a wonderful summer. Ralph had spent most of his time playing with his friends on Carberry Street. He just didn't want the summer to end. School meant getting up early in the morning. School meant doing homework instead of hanging out with friends. Ralph was not happy at the thought of the change. Although, he thought, there was *one* good thing... He would get to see his school friends! He had really missed them over the summer, so he was very happy at the thought of seeing them again.

And there was one other good thing about the end of the summer. His friend Dylan was back!

Dylan showed up on Ralph's doorstep one Saturday morning right before school was due to start. Mom had said they were going to go to the discount store to buy school supplies to prepare for next week. Ralph was in the process of putting on his shoes when he heard a loud knock on the door.

Ralph opened it. "Dylan!" he cried.

Dylan, who had been leaning against the door, literally fell into Ralph's house, laughing and talking nonstop, as usual! Dylan was short and wiry. His last name was Powers. Mom said he was Irish, and that was why had such pale skin. His hair was black and wavy.

Dylan was also extremely funny. He was one of Ralph's best friends. Ralph liked him because he was different. There was absolutely no one else in the world like Dylan, Ralph often thought. And Dylan was so funny when he made jokes - which was all the time! - that he made everyone else seem... well... *boring*.

"I had so much fun in Chicago this summer... more fun than **anyone** ever... while I was in Chicago, I met the top basketball player in the world ... and I ate chocolate ice-cream for breakfast every single morning!" boasted Dylan.

"Really?" Ralph was cautious. As much as he loved Dylan, Ralph knew Dylan was a born storyteller. He would say and do anything for attention, and you never knew what was true and what wasn't. Also, anything anyone said they had done, Dylan would have said he'd done it quicker, bigger, and more often! Because of this, his friends never knew *what* to believe when he started telling stories!

Ralph's dad said Dylan craved attention because his parents were divorced. Dylan's dad left the state after the divorce and hadn't found a job still yet. This meant that Dylan's mom had to work all the time to support the two of them and wasn't at home very much to spend time with Dylan. It did seem to Ralph that Dylan was always in the care of babysitters. That's probably why Mom invited him to stay with their family as much as possible.

Dylan seem to sense his disbelief and was frustrated. "I did! I really did!"

Ralph asked, "When you met the basketball player, did you take pictures?"

Dylan said, "Er... ummm... I didn't have my camera with me! "

"Oh!" said Ralph doubtfully, and moved on to the next subject. "I have to go with my mom to buy school supplies! Want me to ask her if you can come? "

"Yeah!" whooped Dylan.

"Hi Dylan! You're back!" called Mom from the other room. She had instantly recognized Dylan's high-pitched voice. She walked into the room, placing a light pink headband on her head to hold back her long brown hair. "Did you have fun in Chicago this summer? "she asked Dylan.

"I did!" said Dylan. "I just came back on a flight last night. My plane was <u>this big!</u>" he added, opening his arms so wide that he almost fell over again. Ralph laughed at his friend. They all seemed to do quite a lot of laughing when Dylan was around.

Noodle had jumped off the couch and came over to meet Dylan. He sat at Ralph's feet, wagging his tail. "Woof!" He said happily, his brown doggie eyes twinkling up at his new friend.

"Oh, man, Ralphie, you got a dog!" Dylan exclaimed. "And he looks really cool!" he added, leaning over to pat Noodle on the head. He fingered the dog's electric blue collar. Ralph was surprised to see that Noodle took to Dylan as he had rarely taken to anyone! As he watched, Noodle put his head against Dylan's leg and began to make little cooing sounds in his throat. Then he scratched at Dylan's legs in the way that he did when he wanted to be picked up. Even Dylan seemed speechless for once, but he had a huge smile on his face. He simply picked the dog up and said, "I love your dog, Ralph!" Then he sat down on the couch. Noodle jumped up into his lap. At first, Ralph was a little jealous, because ... well... Noodle was *his* dog. But then Ralph noticed the way that Noodle followed Ralph with his eyes, even though he was sitting on Dylan's lap. It was as though he were making sure that Ralph didn't leave the room without him. So, Ralph knew that Noodle did love him. And he was able to quash the little jealous feeling that had sprung up inside him when he saw Noodle sitting on his friend's lap.

Soon, they were in Ralph's family's car, headed to the neighborhood store. During the ride, Dylan regaled them with stories about his summer in Chicago. Ralph noticed his Mom tightened her lips whenever Dylan told a story that was obviously untrue, but at the same time, they were all howling with laughter at Dylan's stories, so it was hard to take him seriously at all. Ralph wondered, though. Sometimes it seemed that Dylan believed his own stories.

I

Ralph thought back and remembered the first time he had met Dylan. Both boys had been four years old. The first thing Dylan had ever said to Ralph was, "I'm Spider Man!" At the time, Ralph had laughed, but thinking back, it did seem to Ralph - even then - that Dylan had believed it himself!

Ralph thought for a moment. He decided to talk to his dad about all of this later. His dad was very smart!

When they arrived at the store, Mom went right to the aisle with for school supplies at the front of the store. The boys raced to the toy section. They passed the dolls and the stuffed animals on the way to the Legos. "Look!" Ralph cried, as he pulled a stuffed dog off the shelves. It was a dachshund, and the toy looked just like Noodle!

Ralph was excited! "I'm going to see if Mom will buy this for me!" he cried.
The boys looked at all the new action figures from the movies they liked. "I have this one at my cousin's house in Chicago!" bragged Dylan, as they looked at the wrestling figures. "And this one... and this one..." Ralph gave him a disgusted look. Sometimes he got tired of

Dylan's bragging, especially when most of the time the things Dylan said weren't true. Dylan didn't even seem to notice, though. He just went right on talking.

That night after dinner, Ralph said, "Dad, can I talk to you?"

Dad looked happy to be asked. He beamed. "Of course, Ralph. What would you like to talk about?" He gestured to the sofa in the living room, and father and son went and sat down together.

"I just can't figure out why Dylan makes up stories all the time!" Ralph told his father. "Do you know? I think he must think that I am really dumb to believe everything he says. And sometimes, it seems like he believes his own stories."

Dad looked very wise, and a little sad. "Ralph, sometimes if people don't like their own life, they make up a different life they wish they had."

Ralph was thoughtful. "Dylan is not happy with his own life, so he makes things up to make it more interesting?" he asked.

Dad continued. "That, and perhaps he really just wants to be liked. You know he doesn't see his father, and his mom doesn't have the time to give him much attention. I think you and I talked about that before. So maybe Dylan is just afraid that other people won't like him, so he makes things up to try to impress other kids - you know, to try to get their attention."

"But he doesn't need to make things up to get people to like him!!" Ralph said, bemused. "He's really nice! And he's so funny!"

Dad's smile was warm. "I think perhaps you need to tell him you feel that way, Ralph. Maybe then he won't worry so much about it." He reached over and tousled his son's hair in that endearing way he had. Ralph loved when his Dad did that.

"Oh, and Ralph," added his father, "Maybe it's not that Dylan thinks you're 'dumb' enough to believe his stories, as you said. I doubt he thinks about it that way at all. I think he just makes up things because he's so desperate for you - and other people - to like him."

"Oh, but guess what, Dad! Noodle really likes Dylan, though!" said Ralph. Noodle perked up at the sound of his name, and Ralph scratched his dog's ears. He told his father about the Noodle's behavior towards his friend earlier that day.

Dad smiled, but again, his smile was a little sad. "Noodle is a very loving dog, Ralph," he said. "Maybe he just somehow understands that Dylan needs that love. They say dogs are very good at figuring out what people are really like. Dogs can sometimes be a very good judge of character." Ralph was thoughtful as he took Noodle to feed him. His Dad had given him a lot to think about.

The next morning at 8:30, Dylan was already at the door. Ralph was still eating his cereal. It was raining that morning, and Dylan didn't have an umbrella or a raincoat. Mom clucked and went to get a towel. "it's really cold and wet out there, Dylan! Why didn't you wear a raincoat?"

"I forgot," said Dylan. "I was there all by myself because the babysitter had to run home for a few minutes," he added. Ralph saw Mom give Dad a "look."

"Well, Dylan, why don't you stay with us today?" asked Dad cheerfully. "Want a bowl of cereal?" Dylan's face lit up. "Yes and Yes!" he said. He parked himself at the kitchen table next to Ralph.

Later, when the boys were watching cartoons, Dylan said, "You're so lucky to have such a cool Mom and Dad! And Noodle," he added, petting the dog who was sprawled between them. He laughed at the way the dog was sprawled out between them with his legs in the air, his head touching Ralph's leg and his tail touching Dylan's!

Ralph grinned at Noodle, too. "Noodle's the best dog ever, anywhere!" he said. But he thought about what his friend had said.

"I never see my mom. Sometimes I don't even think she notices I'm there, when she's home," said Dylan glumly. "She's always so tired."
Dad was walking by the living room on his way upstairs. "Of course, she notices you, Dylan," said Dad gently. "She just has to work a lot so she can take care of you. She loves you. She wants the best for you, and that's why she has to work so much."

"Yeah, she loves you," repeated Ralph. And Ralph thought - How could anyone not love Dylan?

A commercial for a huge water gun came on the television. Dylan looked at Ralph. "I used to have a water gun that was THIS big!" he said, opening his arms as wide as possible. Ralph looked at him, then looked away. He remembered what his dad had said last night. "Dylan, you don't have to make things up all the time," he told his friend. "I like you just the way you are. You don't have to impress me."

Dylan looked a bit touched by Ralph's words, but at the same time, he looked a bit hurt. "I don't make things up! "he said. Then, he seemed to really stop and think about what he had said. Then, he began to look a little guilty. "Well, maybe sometimes... a bit," he admitted.

Ralph said, "Dylan, you tell stories all the time. I never know whether to believe you when you tell me something. And it's not nice!" Ralph added. "It's the same as lying. "

Dylan looked stunned. "Really?"

Ralph nodded. "Yes. And I told you you don't have to do it. Because everyone on Carberry Street likes you anyway. In fact, we know that you make up stories, and we still like you."

Dylan looked speechless. He apparently couldn't think of anything to say. This, Ralph thought, was very unusual. He grinned to himself.

For the rest of the day, as they played, Ralph noticed that Dylan would start to say something - probably to make up a story - but then he would catch himself and stop talking. Therefore, the rest of the day went well. Dylan was his usual funny self, but he didn't tell any lies at all. So, everyone was happy.

That night, Ralph took his bath and got ready for bed, as usual. He lay in bed as usual, with Noodle curled at his feet. His new stuffed dog, the one that looked like Noodle, lay next to him on the bed. Mom had bought it at the store the day she had taken him and Dylan. Ralph slept with it next to him at night.

Mom came in to read Ralph one of his favorite bedtime stories. His favorite stories were from a series about a pack of talking dogs who lived in the same neighborhood and played together. The characters in the book made Ralph think of his friends on Carberry Street.

Ralph told his mom all about what had happened with Dylan that day, and about the talk he'd had with his friend. "...And he stopped making up stories for the rest of the day, anyway, Mom!" he finished.

Mom looked emotional. "Poor Dylan. he's had a bit of a hard life, hasn't he?" She looked as though she were thinking about something. "You know, Ralph, I think we need to ask Dylan's mom if he can stay with us after school and on weekends sometimes. *We* can babysit him," she added. "We can do it for free, and that will save his mother from having to spend money on a babysitter. And maybe she wouldn't have to work as hard if she didn't have to pay a babysitter."

Ralph was ecstatic. "Could we, Mom?! That would be awesome! It would be almost like having a brother!"

His mother smiled. "Yes, it would!" She patted her tummy. "Although don't forget, Ralph, you may *have* a brother soon! Within the next few months, we will find out if your new brother or sister will be a boy or a girl!" His mom had that special glow that she always got when she talked about the new baby.

Ralph thought about her words. "I can't wait to play with my brother or sister, too!" he said. "Maybe Dylan and me and my new brother can play together!"

Mom smiled gently. "Well, Ralph, the baby won't be ready to play with you boys for a while! But I am glad you are looking forward to it."

Mom read Ralph's special book to him. Then she switched off the light. She turned on the plug in-night light, though, to give Ralph a little light, just so it wouldn't get *too* dark in the room. "Good night, honey! "she said affectionately
"Good night, Mom," answered Ralph sleepily. "I love you..." he added, as he floated off to sleep.

Chapter 9: The Bad Attitude

Sam was grumpy when he woke up that morning. It was the first day of school, and Sam - who was usually pretty good-natured - was not in a good mood <u>at all</u>. He hadn't slept well last night because his baby sister, who had been sick the past few days, had cried almost all night. He was miserable about having to go back to school after such a wonderful summer of fun. Also, he had asked Dad for a new LEGO set last night, when he had gone with his family to go buy new school clothes. After all, all of his friends had been able to get this new toy - it had just come out. Sam didn't want to be left out as the only kid who didn't have it. But Sam's dad had said no! "We can't afford it right now!" Dad had explained to him. "We don't have the money for it this week. We already had to come up with extra money for school clothes already. Maybe you'll get it for Christmas. Maybe Santa will bring it!" Dad added reassuringly. But, Sam thought, Christmas was four months away! Was he supposed to wait that long!? It was a *travesty*, he thought, using one of the words he had learned from a video game he'd been playing with Ralph yesterday. Using big words, he found, made him feel very grown up, even if he only said them inside his own head.

In any event, all these terrible happenings had combined to put Sam into a horrible mood! He was scowling as he brushed his teeth and put on the new tan khaki pants they had bought for school last night. In fact, Sam felt like he would never smile again. He thought dramatically, for probably the hundredth time this morning, "I hate my life!"

"If you don't stop frowning, your face is going to freeze that way," Dad teased him. The teasing did nothing to improve Sam's mood.

Angrily, Sam stared at his oatmeal. He didn't want it. At all. Of course they would be out of Lucky Charms cereal again. His mom must have forgotten to get it at the store *again* - she always did. But anyway, it didn't really matter - because he wasn't hungry at all anyway. He felt, or so he told himself, too miserable to eat.

This morning, he just wished he could be anyone - anyone! - else other than himself. He felt like the universe was conspiring against him to make his life totally wretched. Maybe he could stow away on a ship and escape, he thought, ignoring the fact that the nearest ocean was hundreds, if not thousands, of miles away. Or perhaps he could stow away in the baggage compartment of a plane. He could fly to Africa and join a safari and show lions and tigers to tourists all day long. Or maybe the next time the circus came to town, he could run away with it.

"Sam, what is wrong with you?" Mom asked, puzzled, as she drove him to school in the family's van. Sam just scowled even harder. "Nothing," he said shortly. Usually he liked going to his school in the city. He liked the way all the students at his school were different from each other. And he liked the fact that he could have friends who were black, and yellow, and brown, and every color in between. Today, though, there seemed to him to be too many people at his school. He didn't like it, he thought. He wished his school was smaller, and he told his mom so.

"Sam, you are just determined to be unhappy today, aren't you!?" She gave a little smile as though she was amused. His frown grew deeper. *Nobody* understood him, he thought! He wished he had a family that at least cared how he felt. He sighed, feeling very sorry for himself.

After they parked, Mom took him to the front of the school. They had to stop at the office to find out the number of his classroom, as well as to find out who his teacher would be this year. The cheery-looking lady at the front desk smiled at him. He remembered her from last year. "Hello, Sam!" She chirped happily. Oh well, he thought, at least *she* seemed happy to be back. Life sure was easy for grown-ups, he grumbled to himself. They didn't have people bossing them around and telling them what to do all the time. Sam was sure of it! He wished he were a grown-up already.

Mom walked back to see Sam's classroom and meet his new teacher. At the sight of his teacher, Sam decided he didn't like her. She looked mean. He frowned fiercely. He wished he was in the same class as Ralph. He was sure that Ralph had a nice teacher this year! Oh, why couldn't he be in the same class as at least one of his neighborhood friends!? Also, he didn't like the smell of the classroom. It smelled funny to him. It had a rubber smell, like the smell of new erasers. When Sam whispered this to his mom, she responded that perhaps the smell *was* new erasers; after all, they were in a school classroom on the first day of the year. Again, her lips twitched as she responded, and she looked as if she was amused. Sam's mood grew even more sour.

Mom introduced herself to his teacher. Of course, she was her usual bubbly self. Next, she embarrassed Sam by going on and on as the teacher listened, stone-faced, with the whole class listening and staring at them. Before she left, Mom threw her arms around him and hugged him right in front of everyone. Then, she kissed him and wiped away a small tear, as though he were

146

going away on a long trip and she wouldn't see him again for another ten years. "*Mom!!*" he whispered, humiliated. She ignored his words, giving him another tender kiss on the forehead before leaving. He knew he must be twenty shades of red, he thought. He saw his classmates grinning behind their hands, probably thinking about what a '*Momma's boy*' he was. Sam cringed.

Luckily, morning flew by. Lunchtime rolled around, and the class went to the cafeteria to have lunch. They ate spaghetti that day. Sam hated the spaghetti the lunch ladies always served. It tasted like canned SpaghettiOs, which Sam hated! He wished it were pizza day. Even chicken nuggets would have been better than this. He saw Ralph in the cafeteria, but Ralph's class was seated all the way on the other side. Not that it mattered anyway. Since they were in different classes, they would not have been allowed to sit together. And things went on in this gloomy way until after lunch.

After lunch, Sam's new teacher, Mrs. Logsdon, said, "Since it's the first day of school, we're going to do a special activity! This will help us to get to know each other better." Sam groaned inwardly. He didn't like the sound of this! This sounded like one of those "touchy/feely" activities that teachers love to do so much, he thought disgustedly. Especially *girl* teachers, he thought. Yuck.

"Now," said Mrs. Logsdon, "We will go around the room. First, I want you to tell everyone your name and where you are from; and secondly, I want you to tell everyone what you are most thankful for about your life."

Sam racked his brain. How should he answer the question? This *would* happen today, he thought. The one day when he was feeling thankful for absolutely nothing! He decided to listen to his classmates' answers first. Maybe he could get ideas from them.

At first, the activity was uneventful. The first few students gave answers that were fairly normal. One boy said he was thankful for his video games. A friend of Sam's from his class last year, named Mark, told the class he was thankful for his family because they took care of him. At this, Sam thought grouchily that he wished he had a family that took care of him. But his own family only made fun of him! His dad wouldn't even buy him a special toy when he wanted it!

Then a new boy spoke up. Sam had never seen him before, but what he had to say stunned the other students. "I am thankful to be in America, Senora Logsdon!" the boy said in broken English. "The bad men, they took over our town. They shot and killed many people. They shot at my family, too, but we escaped - all but my uncle. They got him." Sam gaped at him. All of the other students were staring at the boy, open-mouthed. Then everyone started talking at once.
"Where did you live?"
"Why did the men shoot everyone?"
"Wow, that sounds like a movie!"
And so on.

Mrs. Logsdon shouted, "Quiet!" Then, everyone stopped talking at once. Very seriously, she said to the boy, "I'm so sorry you had to go through that, Eduardo. That must've been terrible! We, also, are glad that you are here with us now, in a safe place." To the class, she said, "Boys and girls, I do hope you do realize how lucky you are to live here in America! This country might not be perfect, but we have many privileges and freedoms here that people in some other countries do not enjoy."

Sam sat, stunned. Wow, he thought. His life might be tough, he thought, but at least no one was shooting at *his* family. Suddenly his little problems seemed a little more insignificant, and he began to feel a bit silly for being upset this morning.

A beautiful yet prissy little girl went next. Sam stared admiringly at her long, blonde curls. She had a similar answer to Mark's. "I am thankful for my family," she said pertly. Sam thought about that a little more, and he began to thaw out a little. He supposed he was thankful for his family, after all. Even if he did have a baby sister who sometimes cried all night, he groaned to himself.

Another little girl said, "I'm just glad my family has a place to live now." She went on to tell her story. "Last year, my mom and dad couldn't pay the rent, so we got thrown out of our house. I lost my favorite doll, because my mom didn't get it out of the house in time." Now, she sounded like she was about to cry. "My whole family had to share one room at my cousin's house for a while." Sam looked at the girl with sympathy. At least *his* family had enough money that they had never had to be kicked out of their house.

A pert-nosed, brown-haired girl told the group, "I am thankful for my pet hamster. Her name is Sabrina," she added. She seemed to want to go on and on about her hamster, but the teacher stopped her with a smile. "Next?" However, the girl's answer made Sam think of Noodle. Even though Noodle wasn't his own dog, he thought, he loved his best friend's dog anyway. And so, his heart thawed out just a little bit more. By this point, he was almost smiling.

One of the other boys said, "I am thankful for my new video game!" The other one said, "I am grateful for my family's new car, because now I can have a ride to soccer practice without breaking down." The class laughed at this one, although, Sam thought, maybe they shouldn't have. The boy didn't look mad, though. He was smiling too. Then it was Sam's turn.

Sam was beginning to feel better. He supposed this activity was having its intended effect on him, he thought, a little grudgingly. It *was* making him realize just how lucky he really was. A bit gruffly, he said, "I am thankful for my family, my friends, and the people around me. Especially my best friend Ralph. And my baby sister too." Mrs. Logsdon smiled benignly on him and said, "Bravo!" Oh well, maybe she wasn't so mean after all.

After school, Sam waited in front of the school with his friends until his mom arrived to pick him up. When he saw the familiar blue van, he hopped in and gave his mother a heartfelt hug.

She stared at him, stunned. Then she gave him a big grin. "What was that all about?" she asked curiously.

"Just remembering how much I love you, Mom!" said Sam. "And *my* baby sister!" he added proudly. Quickly, he climbed between the front seats of the van so he could go back and give his little sister a kiss, too! She cooed happily at him as he smacked her on the cheek with his lips, then sat in the seat next to her to play with her. He picked up her rattle from the toy box on the floor of the van, and she made a "Gaga!" sound as he waved it in front of her face. He watched as she tried to grasp it with her little hand. "Mom, is the baby feeling better?" he asked curiously. She didn't seem to be coughing as much as she had been last night, he thought.

"Well, you're in a better mood than you were earlier today!" bubbled Mom. "And that makes me extremely happy, I might add!" she teased him. "Sam, the dark looks... the scowling face... it's just not... you! I'm so very happy to have my sunny little boy back!"

Then, in answer to his question, she said: "The baby seems a little better today! I took her to the doctor right before I came to pick you up, so I still haven't had a chance to sleep yet. When we get home, I'll put her down for a nap, then try to catch a little sleep myself on the couch."

Again, Sam felt a little guilty about his attitude this morning. He thought of how hard his mom worked to take care of their family. He decided he needed to tell his mother the whole story of his day, starting with his bad morning, and ending with the class exercise. As he told her, she listened, stopping him every now and then to ask a question.

"Well, Sam," she said seriously, "It sounds like you were suffering from a serious case of a bad attitude. That's what sometimes happens when you get too wrapped up in yourself!" She continued, "This morning, did you ever stop to think about how any of the rest of us were feeling? Do you think the baby enjoyed being sick? Do you suppose your father felt good about having to say no to you about the toy? And, I can tell you, I was not happy to be up all night with the baby either! I am exhausted today. But you never stopped to think about that, did you?"

Sam started to speak, to defend himself, but his mom held up her hand as if to stop him. "Sam, I really do understand," she said. "But, the next time something like this happens - and you are tempted to feel sorry for yourself -simply focus on someone else. Try to focus on the way other people feel. Or try to help someone, even! It will take your mind off yourself and put it on other things. Before you know it, you won't have the energy to feel sorry for yourself anymore! Because, Sam," Mom said emphatically, "It takes a lot of energy to feel sorry for yourself."

Sam thought of his attitude this morning, and of how miserable he had been. "Yes, it does," he agreed.
Their van turned the corner onto Carberry Street. Sam asked, "Mom, want me to bring the playpen into the living room so we can put the baby down for a nap?"

asked Sam. "I can keep an eye on the baby while she naps. That way, you can sleep better."

Mom gave him a big smile. "That would be wonderful, Samuel!" she answered, calling him by his full name, the way she always did when she was pleased with something he had done or said.

Sam was happy to be home. It had been a rough day for him; however, he felt he was coming home to the house much wiser than he had left it this morning!

With a contented sigh, Sam settled down to watch cartoons while his mom and baby sister slept.

Chapter 10: A Special Thanksgiving

Before Ralph knew it, autumn had raced by. The days were becoming shorter, and the red and yellow leaves were falling from the trees. Halloween came to Carberry Street, and the children put on their costumes and went trick or treating around the neighborhood. Then November arrived with its cold, blustery weather. Suddenly, it was almost Thanksgiving. One Saturday morning near the end of November, Ralph and Dylan went to the grocery store with Ralph's mother to help her buy the food for their "Thanksgiving feast." This was how Dad referred to their annual Thanksgiving dinner. It was always a special dinner because Ralph's mom and Dad would invite people for the holiday who didn't have anywhere else to spend Thanksgiving, or who didn't have family in the area. Sometimes, they would just invite people that they liked. So, the family almost always had a full table at Thanksgiving.

Ralph was excited because Dylan and his mother were coming to spend Thanksgiving with them! Ralph's new teacher, who had only been living in the city for a few months, was also coming over on Thanksgiving. Ralph liked his new teacher. He missed his first teacher, but Mr. O'Mara was awesome! He liked the same things the boys in class did, like Pokémon and Beyblades. Sometimes in science class, they would do killer science experiments because Mr. O'Mara was also a scientist who liked to, as he put it, "Blow things up." He wasn't married, and he didn't have any kids, which Ralph thought was a shame because he would have made a *perfect* Dad! He even paid extra attention to Dylan because he had heard that Dylan didn't see his Father very much, and that his mother worked all the time. Mr. O'Mara even had a cabinet with cereal and other snacks that kids liked. If a student forgot his lunch, did not have time to eat breakfast, or even didn't have food at home, he or she would be allowed to pick something from the cabinet. More than once he had helped Ralph out when he forgot his lunch money. Mr. O'Mara had let him take a cheese wedge, an apple, and even a bag of chips from the cabinet. Dylan, too, was sometimes allowed to choose from the cabinet too, especially right before his mom's payday, when there wasn't much to eat at his house.

That day at the grocery store, the boys helped Ralphs mom pick out a giant turkey, a glazed ham, and lots of potatoes. They picked up several bags of bread crumbs to make stuffing. Mom got sweet potatoes too, and she let the boys choose a few pies from the bakery! Ralph picked his favorite kind of pie... Pumpkin pie! Dylan, on the other hand, liked apple pie the best, so he chose an especially big one. Then, they rounded off their trip with a trip to the ice cream aisle to get vanilla ice cream. Ralph looked at the buggy. Something was still missing! He reminded his mom that they had whipped cream every year for the pumpkin pie. His mother gasped. "Oh, no! I can't believe I almost forgot the whipped cream! That's a family tradition!" She added to Ralph, "I think you like the whipped cream even better than the pumpkin pie!"

Ralph thought about it. "It's close!" he grinned. He liked to be able to pile a huge mound of whipped cream on top of his pumpkin pie. Mom picked up three cartons of

Cool Whip whipped cream and put them into the shopping cart. Ralph's mouth watered at the mere sight of it. "Don't you be sneaking into it before Thanksgiving!" His mother said knowingly. Ralph grinned to himself. There was just something about mothers! They knew what kind of trouble you were spoiling to get into before you even knew it yourself!

At the checkout counters, Ralph and Dylan unloaded the food onto the counter so the cashier could ring it up. "Hello, boys!" said the blonde lady behind the counter. Ralph remembered her. When they came to the grocery store, she often helped them. She looked at Mom. "Well, don't you have some good helpers today?" she said, smiling. She looked at Mom's stomach, which, thought Ralph, was really starting to stick out. "Isn't the baby due soon?" She asked Ralph's mother frankly.

Mom got that special glow she always had when she talked about the baby. "He'll be coming along in a few months," she said happily. She had found out at the doctor's that the baby was going to be a boy.

The lady looked at Ralph and raised her eyebrows. "It's your last Christmas as an only child, Ralph! How do you feel about that?"

Ralph smiled back. He was excited about the baby! He thought having a brother would be more interesting than if it were a sister. "I wasn't sure at first, but I decided I want it after all. So, I don't mind!" He said, a bit magnanimously, feeling he was doing his mom a favor by being so accepting of the change. Both ladies laughed. Ralph's feelings were hurt. He couldn't figure out why adults always laughed when he said things like that. He meant them seriously.

The cashier, though, looked as though she were being entertained. As they left, she handed them each a chocolate bar from the rack next to the cash register. "It's on me," she smiled, pulling a few dollar bills out of the pocket of her uniform and putting it in the register. "Hey, thanks!" The boys chorused, while mom smiled her usual gentle smile and thanked the lady, as well. The boys felt very grown-up as they pushed the cart out to the family's car and loaded the groceries in the trunk. Ralph had been working hard to help Mom; while she was pregnant, Dad wanted her to do as little work as possible. He had a talk with Ralph about this a few months ago. So, Ralph had been trying to be responsible and help Mom out as much as possible.

When they arrived home, Ralph and Dylan helped Mom to put their special Thanksgiving groceries away. Ralph put the turkey and ham into the refrigerator, where they took up most of the room on the shelf. Next, he stacked the whipped cream cartons and put them on the bottom shelf. He tried not to look at them, but he couldn't help but think how good the whipped cream would taste. But he knew that if he opened one of the cartons, Mom would be angry. So, he suffered in silence.

It seemed more silent than usual in the house today. Ralph noticed that his friend was a little quiet this afternoon. In fact, now that he thought about it, Dylan had been a little subdued today. He did not seem as happy as usual. "What's wrong, Dylan?" He asked. He found that he missed his friend's usual exuberance.

Dylan looked bothered. "I'm kind of worried about my mom," he said.

"What's wrong?" Ralph asked, concerned.

Dylan frowned. "She seems really sad all the time. Sometimes I hear her crying at night. Also, sometimes she calls my dad, and then they fight and then she cries more. It just seems like lately, she cries all the time."

Ralph was sad. He felt sorry for both Dylan and his mother. "Maybe I can tell Mom," he said, feeling that his mom could fix just about any problem. "Maybe she will talk to your mom when she's here on Thanksgiving."

Dylan's expression lightened a little. "That would be great!" He smiled. Apparently Dylan had the same confidence in Ralph's mom that Ralph did, because he seemed much happier after that. Or maybe, thought Ralph, Dylan was just glad to have someone try to help him and his mom.

That night, Ralph woke up in the middle of the night. He was hungry, and all he could think about was the whipped cream in the refrigerator downstairs. Was it possible that Mom wouldn't notice if he opened it and ate just a little bit? Of course she would notice, he thought. She would notice immediately! But all he could think about was how much better he would feel if he could just eat a little bit of it. He *was* hungry, after all. And maybe she wouldn't get that mad, he told himself.

Ralph tiptoed down the stairs to the kitchen, Noodle at his heels. The poor dog looked confused. They did not usually come downstairs in the middle of the night. Ralph took the Cool Whip out of the refrigerator. He knew this would be his last time to turn back! But the way that he felt right now seemed much more important than consequences that he wouldn't have to deal with until later. And once he opened it, he couldn't stop. He ate the whole container.

Afterward, he was consumed by guilt. And just then, he remembered that the other day Mom had also said something about his weight! She said he had been eating too much lately. But Ralph felt that when something tasted good, it was hard for him to stop eating. He supposed that was just the way he was.

Now his stomach was hurting. He decided to go back to bed. What could he do with the container? If he put it in the trash can, his mom might see it. He took the container back upstairs and hid it in the back of his closet. Now, he thought, he felt even more guilty than before. He was dreading the next morning, when Mom would surely notice that the whipped cream was gone. He wondered what would happen tomorrow, and as he did so, he fell into an uneasy sleep.

To his surprise, however, Mom didn't notice the missing carton of whipped cream the next day. Or the next day.

Or the next day after that! Ralph couldn't believe it. But he continued to feel bad and to dread the day when his mom did notice. Surely she would eventually. When he thought about it, he got a hollow feeling in the bottom of his stomach. And the feeling seemed to get worse with every day that went by.

Thanksgiving morning dawned cold, yet sunny. Ralph just loved holidays! The house just seemed to crackle with a wonderful excitement. Mom had gotten out of bed early to start baking, so succulent smell of turkey was already wafting through the house. And, best of all, there was no school today! Ralph poured himself a bowl of cereal and settled down to watch TV. Suddenly, he heard a cry of surprise from the kitchen. He winced. With all the excitement this morning, he had almost forgotten about the whipped cream. He screwed his eyes shut and waited for it...

"RALPH! Come in this kitchen right now, please!" Mom's voice sounded clipped - the way it always did when she was trying to control her anger.

Slowly, Ralph rose and shuffled, reluctantly, into the kitchen. He was not looking forward to this.

His mother was staring at him, open-mouthed. "Ralph, you ate that whole carton of whipped cream!"

Ralph stared at the floor. He felt the tears coming, but he tried not to give into them. He knew he had made a mistake. All he could think of to say was, "I was hungry, Mom."

Ralph chanced a quick look at her face. She still looked disturbed, but he could tell she was recovering from the surprise. "When did this happen!?" she asked.

"The night we bought it," Ralph answered.

"I can't believe I didn't notice until this morning," mused Mom. But now, she didn't sound mad anymore. Rather, she sounded disappointed.

"Well, Ralph," said Mom, "We will talk more about this tonight. Let's not let it ruin our holiday! But please know, Ralph," she went on, "That I don't care so much about not having the whipped cream. What I care about is you, and there are a few different things that bother me about this! But you and I will talk later this evening," she concluded.

Was she finished? Ralph couldn't believe that would be it. But she gave him one final concerned look, then turned back around to the stove to finish making the stuffing. "We'll be eating at noon," she added to him over her shoulder. "Since we are having company today, put on a clean shirt, Ok Ralph?" He nodded and went upstairs to his room. He put on his favorite red polo shirt. Then he heard a knock on the door. Someone opened it, and then he heard Dylan's voice!

"Dylan!" said Ralph, racing down the stairs. The grown-ups laughed as Noodle threw himself at Dylan as if he hadn't seen him in weeks - instead of just yesterday afternoon, which was the case! Dylan turned around to talk to someone just outside the door, and Ralph saw his mom behind him. He saw someone else, too. Mr. O'Mara was already with them.

Ralph's first thought was that Dylan's mom didn't *look* upset. She was laughing and talking to Mr. O'Mara, who, Ralph thought, was looking at her as though he hadn't ever seen a girl before. Dylan didn't seem to notice. He was back to his usual hyper self. "Mom, look how Noodle loves me! He always jumps on me like this."

"That's so sweet, honey!" said his Mom. "What a cute little dog!" She added, bending to pet Noodle herself.

"Roof! Roof!" Said Noodle, with a strange, stifled bark that sounded suspiciously like "Thank You!" The adults laughed again.

Mom was looking at Dylan's mom and Mr. O'Mara. "Do you all know each other?" she asked curiously.

"He gave Dylan a ride home from school yesterday when the babysitter couldn't pick him up," Dylan's mom responded. She was looking down, but Ralph would swear that she was blushing. Mom nodded and a small smile popped up on her lips. She looked very interested.

"Well, food's almost ready," said Dad. "Let's get this party started!"

Ralph thought that, despite the rough start to the morning, it turned out to be a wonderful day after all. Everyone was happy just to be together. They all ate turkey and stuffing and sweet potatoes. Afterwards, they polished it off with the pie and ice-cream. Ralph had never felt so full in his life!

That night, after Ralph went to bed, Mom came in to kiss him goodnight. "Ralph," she said worriedly, "First of all, you've been eating too much lately. You need to start being more careful about what you eat. It was bad enough that you snuck and opened up the whipped cream, but you shouldn't be eating a whole carton of anything like that. Not taking care of your body will make you sick."

"I know, Mom," said Ralph, ashamed.

"Now," said Mom, more sternly, "The other issue here is that you snuck and did something that you knew you were not supposed to do. For that, your father is going to ground you tomorrow. I don't care how hungry you say you were, there is absolutely no excuse to behave like that."

"I know, Mom," said Ralph. He felt ashamed.

"Promise me you won't do it again, Ralph," said his mother.

"I won't," Ralph said honestly. And he told his mom how he had been worried every day that she would find out.

"So, your conscience has been bothering you. That's actually good!" Said Mom.

"What's a conscious?" Ralph asked.

"*Conscience*," corrected his Mom. "Ralph, your conscience is something in your mind that bothers you when you do something wrong. You should always listen to your conscience! It's there to help you."

"OK, Mom," said Ralph. He was relieved the whole thing was over.

"Good night, Ralph!" Said mom, bending down to give him a kiss on the head. " and "Good night, Noodle!" She added, bending over to give him a kiss on the head, too!

"Woof!" Said Noodle.

Chapter 11: Christmas on Carberry Street

Dylan's Wish / The Christmas Play

"It's beginning to look a lot like Christmas," crooned the smooth voice of the singer from the stereo. The holiday music wafted through the house, creating a festive atmosphere as Ralph, Dylan, and Sam helped Ralph's mom to take the Christmas decorations from the big box where they had stored them last year and put them up in the house. It was the weekend after Thanksgiving, and preparations for the Christmas holidays were in full swing.

Dylan and Ralph were hanging Christmas ornaments - many of them collected throughout past years - on the Christmas tree. Ralph saw the ornament his parents had bought to celebrate the year he was born. It was a baby angel with the date of his birth on it. There was even one that celebrated the year his parents got married. It was a set of gold rings wrapped around a Christmas tree with the date of their wedding in fancy writing in the middle. He looked more closely at the ornament and found that it was 10 years in the past, which seemed eons ago to Ralph. It was hard for Ralph to imagine that his parents had existed even before he was born. He just couldn't picture it! He wondered how they had spent their time without him. Maybe sometime he would ask them, he thought.

The Christmas tree they had bought this year was beautiful. Ralph and his dad had gone to a Christmas tree lot near their house and picked out a real tree, the same way they had done every year, as far back as Ralph could remember. Ralph knew his mom did not like fake Christmas trees; whenever she saw one, she would wrinkle her nose, frown, and say, "It's just not the same!" So, every year, they had to have a new Christmas tree. Ralph had come to associate the smell of a new pine tree with Christmas time.

Noodle sat on the floor near Ralph. His tail wagged happily as he watched the action unfold around him. An old red bow, left over from last year's gift wrap, hung off the side of his head. Sam had laughingly placed it there after pulling it out of a box of Christmas decorations earlier that afternoon. Noddle hadn't minded, though. He always loved any kind of attention. Noodle was a good sport, Ralph thought proudly. And the bow looked really cool on him!

Emily was there too, but Ralph noticed she was unusually quiet today. She sat off to the side in her wheelchair - Ruby, of course, sat possessively on her lap. Ralph noted, however, that Emily was happy. In fact, he thought, amused, right now she and Ruby were wearing matching smiles. Nobody could grin like Ruby. Ralph had never seen a dog that had such a big grin. And Emily and her dog were very in tune with each other, he thought. The two of them always seemed to be doing the same thing at the same time. Ralph thought about how Noodle having had added to the lives of his family and friends this year. The dogs on Carberry Street seemed to contribute so much love to all of their families' lives. And they all had such a neat little personality.

As if reading his thoughts, Noodle came over and brushed against his leg. He sat at Ralph's feet and looked up at him adoringly. Ralph smiled back at him. "I'm so glad you came to live with us this year, Noodle!" said Ralph. "Yip!" responded Noodle happily.

Ralph's mom smiled at him. Right now, she was sitting on the couch, pulling Christmas decorations out of the box. "Having Noodle has really made a difference in our family this year, hasn't it?" She seemed to be following the way Ralph was thinking. Not for the first time, Ralph was awed by the way that his mom seemed to be able to read his mind. Her next words, though, pulled him out of his thoughts. "We should do something nice for the doggies this Christmas. Maybe we will get Noodle and Ruby each a present from the pet store! I'm sure they would like to have some big bones, or maybe even some toys to chew on."

"That would be awesome!" cried Ralph. "And Noodle needs a new collar. Maybe a yellow one," he added.

Yellow was kind of a sunny color, thought Ralph. It would fit Noodle's personality very well!

"Arf!" smiled Noodle. Apparently he approved. Ruby's response to all of this was to gaze at both Ralph and his Mom with shining eyes.

Mom pulled some silver tinsel with hanging red bows from the box. Using scotch tape, she began to hang it carefully over the fireplace. She turned around to get more tinsel out of the box and smiled at Ralph when she saw him watching her. "This time next year you will have a little brother! "She reminded him. "We will have to be sure to get a new ornament for the tree next year to celebrate his birth!" So, Ralph knew that, next Christmas, there would be a baby ornament hanging on the tree with his new brother's name and birthdate on it. In future years, he would look at it and remember her birth, just as he had looked at the ornament today which had celebrated his own birth. He wondered if, someday, more ornaments would hang on the tree for future brothers and sisters. His parents always said that they wanted to have at least three children. If so, he would get to be an older brother again and again! And he would always have at least one brother or sister at home to play with. It was an exciting thought.

Emily may have been quiet today, but the truth was that she was thinking hard. She was quite happy with her life now. Looking back, it seemed silly to think how worried she had been about moving to the city. In the end, this had turned out to be an amazing year. She had moved to an exciting new home and made some really cool friends. She had her family and, of course, her loyal little dog Ruby to snuggle with whenever she felt like she needed affection. In fact, Emily decided that she would not change a thing about her life right now, even if she had the chance.

Sam was trying to find a way to put the pretty little glittering angel on the top of the tree. He thought that he could probably get Ralph's mom to do it, but he really wanted to do it himself. He pulled a chair over from the dining room table and climbed on top of it. There! It was done. The angel beamed down from the top of the tree. Now the tree was finished. He looked down at his friend Dylan, who was talking so excitedly and distractedly about the toy he wanted for Christmas that he almost fell into the tree. Sam was amused and exasperated at the same time. It was so typical of his friend. "Dylan, can you please be careful? We just spent a half hour putting the tree up, and you are going to knock the whole thing over in two seconds," he groused. Dylan ignored him, as he often did when someone said something he didn't want to hear.

Sam was happy this Christmas too. His mom had promised to buy him the new Lego set he wanted for Christmas. He was also excited because, over the Christmas break, his family was going to go visit his Uncle Brian and Aunt Tansy in New York State. That meant that Sam was going to get to go on a plane. Sam loved riding in planes! He loved the feeling of riding as high up as a bird and looking down at the clouds below. When he grew up, he thought he might want to be a pilot.

As for Dylan, he was feeling over the moon this holiday season. Just this morning, his mom's new friend, Mr. O'Mara had said that Dylan could call him Bob now. Dylan was ecstatic. Mr. O'Mara... Bob... was also Dylan's teacher at school, and he was one of the coolest people Dylan had ever met! Dylan's mom had explained to him, very gently, that she had "gone out" with Mr. O'Mara a few times. She looked happier than Dylan remembered ever seeing her before. All Dylan could do was hope that Bob would be his new dad. He wondered if there was something, he could do to help make it happen! He really would like to have a dad, and Bob would make a neat dad, thought Dylan. He always listened to Dylan... *really* listened. And he truly looked interested in what Dylan had to say. He didn't have that distracted look that adults sometimes got when they pretended to be listening to you, but you knew they were really thinking about something else. Plus, Bob loved to do science experiments. None of Dylan's friends had a dad who wanted to do things like that! They were all into things like watching the football game or reading the newspaper. Those things were OK, Dylan supposed, but they certainly weren't nearly as much fun as the stuff Bob liked to do. It was almost like having another kid to play with. He supposed this must be what it was like when you had a teacher for a dad. He had tried to say something to his mom about all of this, but she just sorts of turned red and mumbled that you couldn't rush things before she quickly started talking about something different. But maybe, thought Dylan, maybe there was something he could do to make Bob want to stay for good! The first chance he got, he decided to pull Ralph aside and see if he had any ideas. For Dylan had decided that what he wanted for his Christmas present this year was to have Mr. O'Mara for a father.

He didn't get the chance until later, after Emily and Sam had gone home. When he asked Ralph, his friend looked a little dubious. "I don't know, Dylan. That sounds like one of those movies you see where the kids try to set the parents up, but then everything kind of falls apart and it never works."

Dylan laughed. "There must be something we can do, though!" he said.

Ralph was thoughtful. "Maybe you can get him to sign a contract?" he said.

Dylan was dubious. "A contract?"

"Well," Ralph said, "Like, when my parents got their car, they had to sign a contract. And when they bought a washing machine, they had to sign a contract. It seems like you can get things you want by signing a contract. But I guess you would have to promise Mr. O'Mara something. Like money."

Dylan's face fell. "I don't really have any money though. I might when I grow up, though!" His face brightened a little. "Maybe he would wait and let me pay him then?"

Just then, Ralph's mother came around the corner. She must have been listening from the other room, Dylan thought. "What's all this talk about contracts?" She asked curiously.

"Dylan really wants Mr. O'Mara to be his dad, so we were trying to think of a way to set up a contract," Ralph explained.

Mom looked like she was trying hard not to laugh. "Boys, contracts don't exactly work that way," she explained. She started to explain further, but the doorbell rang. Noodle started to bark. Ralph ran downstairs, Noodle at his heels, because he thought it might be one of his friends. But he saw it was just a delivery man handing his mom a package. After that, mom forgot what they had been talking about. And Ralph went back upstairs to play with Dylan.

Dylan didn't forget though. But he decided to talk to Mr. O'Mara... Bob... about it next week at school.

He had his chance in PE class the next week. The students were having free play, and Dylan was throwing a ball with Ralph and a few other boys. He looked over and saw his teacher walking down the sidewalk, getting ready to pick up their class from PE. This seemed like the perfect opportunity to talk to him!

Dylan ran over to him. "Can you be my dad, Bob?" he asked honestly. His teacher first looked shocked, then turned several shades of red. Dylan was surprised. Maybe he should've said hello first, he thought. "Uh, hi, Bob," he amended.

Bob looked at him gently. He leaned his tall, rangy body against the brick wall behind him as he thoughtfully rubbed his head. "Dylan, buddy, I think at school, you should probably still call me Mr. O'Mara." Reassuringly, though, he winked at Dylan. "And this isn't really a good time or place for this conversation, OK? Let's talk more about this after school."

"Ok," said Dylan, disappointed. But, he thought, at least his teacher hadn't said "No." he went back and played ball with his friends for a few more minutes until his PE teacher, Mrs. Zeller, yelled "Let's Line Up!" Then the class followed their teacher back to the classroom.

"How did it go?" Ralph whispered, as they went back to their seats. Dylan shrugged and put his palms up.

After school, though, Dylan stayed behind after his friends left to go home. Mr. O'Mara looked at Dylan. "Let's sit down over here" he said, gesturing to a table in the back of the room. Then, he proceeded to say to Dylan pretty much the same thing that Dylan's mom had told him: These things took time.

"But I really wanted you as a dad. I wanted that for Christmas," Dylan explained. "I could be a really good son to you," he added. As he said this, to his humiliation, he heard his own voice start to break a little, as unshed tears rose to the surface. Fiercely, he wiped one away. He didn't want to cry. But he continued to plead his case. "I tried to be a good son to my dad. I don't know why he left," he added.

Mr. O'Mara looked sad. "Dylan," he said, "Sometimes things just don't work out between moms and dads. It doesn't mean that you did anything wrong. I'm sure you were a great son."

"And I really like your mom," he added. "She's a really nice lady. But you see, Dylan, can't force things like that to happen just because you want them to. Sometimes you just have to wait and let them happen on their own. And when - or if - they are meant to happen, they will."

Dylan still felt like he might cry. He had been very happy at the idea of having his teacher for a father. Mr. O'Mara looked at him as though he wasn't sure what to say. Eventually, though, he said, "Dylan, I promise I will always be here for you. Whether or not things work out between your mother and I, you can think of me as a substitute father. Ok? I promise to always be there for you when you need anything, or if you even just want someone to talk to."

Now, Dylan felt like he might cry again, but this time they were happy tears. "Really? You promise not to leave me?" he asked.

He looked at Mr. O'Mara. Now, he thought, his teacher looked like he was the one who might be about to cry. "Of course I won't leave you, Dylan," he answered, in a kind way. "Why would I do that? You're such a great kid!"

"I am? You think so?" Dylan felt as if a load had been lifted off him. He smiled.

"Now," said Mr. O'Mara, unfolding his long legs from off the little classroom chair, "Important things first! Let's go get some ice cream! After that, I'll give you a ride home."

"Ice cream, yay!" Said Dylan. "Can I get chocolate chip cookie dough? That's my favorite!!"

"Of course! You can get ANY kind you want!" said his teacher, as he held the door open for Ralph. Together, the two of them walked out into the chilly autumn afternoon. As they walked down the sidewalk toward the parking lot, Mr. O'Mara reached over and affectionately rumpled his hair.

Back at Carberry Street, though, Emily was feeling far less happy. She had just arrived home from school, and she was telling her mom about her day. There was going to be a Christmas musical at school, and every class was going to do a different skit and sing. But Emily didn't have a part. Emily *never* had a part in any of these things. She hadn't been chosen to be in the fall musical, either, several months ago. It was as though people completely left her out of everything because she was in a wheelchair. She was tired of it, and she felt very left out. It was a constant theme in her life; it happened over and over again.

Even Ralph, she thought, was going to be in the play. Since he was chubby, he had been chosen to play Santa

Claus. Of course, he didn't want to. Most of the boys were not very excited about being in the musical. But Emily would have gladly traded places with any one of them.

Emily's mom looked very sad. "I'll send a note to the teacher!" she told Emily.

Emily frowned. "You shouldn't have to, though!" She answered sulkily. "And it's not just this time, either! Everyone always forgets about me. I'm never included in anything." Unbidden, a small tear found its way down her cheek.

Sensing her mood, Ruby jumped up into her lap and started to lick her hand. She kissed Emily's face, too. Well, I love you! She seemed to be saying. Emily hugged her close. She was so glad she had Ruby for a pet.

After a few minutes, Mom pushed Emily into the living room so she could watch television for a few minutes before dinner. Emily looked at the sitcom without really paying attention to it. She was thinking about her dream. For Emily had a dream that, one morning, she would wake up and be able to walk again, like the other students in her class could. And, instead of her straight yellow, somewhat nondescript hair, she would have beautiful corn-colored colors like the prettiest girl in her class, Heather Collins. Not only was Heather beautiful, but she was always picked first for everything. And all of the boys wanted to be her boyfriend, too, thought Emily. Heather seemed to lead a charmed life.

Emily sighed. She knew her dream would never come true! She would wake up tomorrow morning and still be the same old Emily that she had always been. In the same old wheelchair! She just knew that nothing was going to change in her life. The thought made her even sadder.

There was a knock on the door. Emily's mom opened it and said cheerfully, "Hi, Ralph!"

Usually a visit from Ralph could cheer Emily up. Today, though, she doubted if even that could pull her out of her doldrums.

"Hi, Emily!" said Ralph happily. He stopped talking at the sight of her angry face. "What's wrong?" he asked curiously.

"I don't get to be in the Christmas show," answered Emily. "And almost everyone else in the class gets to do it! "

Ralph looked bothered. "You can have my part," he offered generously. "But I don't want it anyway," he added, quite honestly. At this, Emily almost smiled. Ralph was so funny!

"I'm always left out of everything!" Emily said sulkily. "I wish I could be like the other girls. Like Heather Collins. She always gets asked to do everything! She has the lead role in the play."

Ralph looked surprised. "Heather Collins!? REALLY?" he said doubtfully. "Oh, please, Emily! You're way nicer than Heather Collins. She's... well, not to be mean... but she's kinda stuck up. She always seems... I don't know... fake."

Emily was surprised. "You think so?"

Ralph nodded sagely. "Yeah. And she's not that nice, either. Not like you," he added. "I'm glad you're not Heather, because then you wouldn't be Emily. And there is a lot of special things about you, Emily, that Heather definitely doesn't have," he said loyally.

Emily was really touched. "Thanks, Ralph!" she said softly. She grew a little misty-eyed. Not for the first time, she thought of how lucky she was to have a good friend like Ralph! When she felt bad, he always tried to make her feel better. He was always trying to help other people, too. She decided that *Ralph* was the kind of person that she would like to be. Maybe she didn't really want to be like Heather Collins, after all. But she did still want to be in the Christmas show, and she said as much to Ralph.

Ralph was alert. She could tell he was thinking hard. "I have an idea. Why don't you just go and talk to your teacher? Why don't *we* go and talk to your teacher?"

"You'd come with me, Ralph?"

He nodded. "I would, sure!"

Emily was a little doubtful. "My mom said she was going to call. I'm not sure if we should go and talk to a teacher about something like that, Ralph."

Ralph looked puzzled. "Why?"

Emily hedged a little. "Well... I don't know. She might think we are criticizing her or something."

Ralph considered, then he shook his head. "I don't think so. Not if we say it the right way." He paused. "Also,

Emily, you might be wrong. Mrs. Payne seems awfully nice. Maybe she has a reason for not including you."

Emily was a little scornful. "I'm not sure what could be a good reason for excluding someone from a class Christmas show. Besides," she felt compelled to add, "This happens all the time. It's not just this one time that's bothering me."

Ralph looked at her sentimentally. "Well, Emily, then I think we need to start standing up for you whenever it happens. To be fair," he added reasonably, "Maybe people don't realize they are doing it."

Emily blinked. She hadn't thought of that. She had just assumed people were excluding her on purpose. And she liked the way that Ralph had said "we." As though they were a team, she thought. After their talk, Emily felt better. When her mom came into the room, they told her what they had decided to do.

Emily's mom looked gratefully at Ralph. "Well, if you're sure!" was all she said. Emily knew that her mom thought a lot of Ralph. He was a good boy, she often said. After all, it was he and Sam that had raised enough money to get Emily a new wheelchair.

Before Ralph went home that evening, he and Emily decided to go talk to Mrs. Payne the next day.

The next morning was cold and cloudy. Emily felt nervous as her mom brushed her hair and got her ready for school. She didn't say anything to her mom, but that was how she was feeling inside. What if her teacher became angry?

All day long, she dreaded the meeting. She avoided meeting her teacher's eyes as much as possible. She caught Mrs. Payne looking at her strangely a few times. She seemed to sense that something was wrong. By the end of the day, Emily had a nervous feeling in her stomach. She thought, "I just can't wait to get this over." When the bell rang, signaling the end of the school day, she felt very relieved. Just about an hour from now, she thought, this would all be over with and she would be home with her mother.

She waited by the door of her classroom for Ralph to come and meet her. Suddenly, the classroom door opened, and Mrs. Payne came out!

"Is everything OK, Emily?" she asked curiously.

Emily forced a smile to her face. "Sure! Everything is fine," she said. "Ummm... Mrs. Payne... can we talk to you for a minute?"

Her teacher looked around, confused. "We?"

"Ralph is coming," Emily explained.

Mrs. Payne looked even more confused. "Emily, what is this about? I have to go to a rehearsal for the school play," she explained.

Emily's face cleared a little. "Perfect! We wanted to talk to you about the school play."

Mrs. Payne nodded. "Well, come to the cafeteria when he gets here, ok?" she said, in her usual no-nonsense way.

"Thanks, Mrs. Payne," said Emily softly. She hoped to Ralph was right, and this was all a misunderstanding. Mrs. Payne really did seem like a nice person, she thought.

After a few minutes, Ralph came racing down the hall, trailed by a harried-looking Dylan who was - as always! - talking away about a mile a minute. Emily smiled. Dylan was always such a mess that he always seemed to arouse some mothering instinct in her. "How are you today, Dylan?" she asked him kindly.

Dylan looked at her, a little askance. "I lost my Math homework today! It fell out of my binder somehow," he said. "I'm going to get into so much trouble!"

Ralph grinned at Emily. "I'm going to try to help him find it tomorrow," he told her confidentially. "He probably dropped it in the hall on the way to class, or something like that. Maybe someone found it and took it to the office. Or maybe he even dropped it in his Mom's car this morning. Or left it at home." The three of them went down the hall and entered the cafeteria through the big steel doors. Emily saw people from her class on the stage practicing their lines. There were people from some of the other classes sitting in the seats and watching the rehearsal, as well. Once again, Emily felt left out.

Mrs. Payne came over to them immediately. "Emily, what is going on?" she asked. Suddenly, Emily couldn't speak. She had lost her nerve! She looked mutely at Ralph. Immediately, he smiled at her reassuringly.

"Mrs. Payne," he told her earnestly, "I don't know if you know who I am, but I live near Emily on Carberry Street."

"Of course I know who you are, Ralph!" Mrs. Payne smiled at him. "You're the boy who raised money to buy Emily a new wheelchair last summer. You are a bit of a legend!" she teased him.

Ralph preened a little, but then he shrugged. "Well, honestly though, we didn't do that much! All we did was set up a lemonade stand. Then someone saw us on the news and donated a wheelchair anyway."

Mrs. Payne smiled at him. "Your humility is admirable, Ralph. But go on."

Emily wanted to giggle. Knowing Ralph as she did, she could tell that he was trying to remember what the word "humility" meant. Apparently, he tried and failed, because he went on, "Ok. So anyway. Last night I went down the street to hang out with Emily, and she was really sad because she was feeling left out. She really wants to be in the school play, or show, or whatever it's called this year."

Dylan perked up. "She does? She can have my part," he said. Emily couldn't help it. She giggled. It was the exact same thing that Ralph had said last night.

Mrs. Payne looked surprised. "You want to be in the show, Emily? Why didn't you just say something to me?" she asked.

Again, Ralph spoke for her. "She just felt bad because she felt like she was being excluded."

Mrs. Payne looked at Emily. "Thank you, Ralph, but let Emily speak for herself this time."

Emily spoke very softly. She felt very shy about expressing her innermost feelings to an adult - even a teacher - that she didn't know very well. "I always feel like I'm left out of everything. Because I'm in a wheelchair."

Mrs. Payne looked as though she had been clubbed over the head. She looks like she had never, ever in her life thought of anything like this. "Emily, no! Please don't think like that! No one was deliberately leaving you out of anything! It's just..." she hesitated. "Well, Emily... I guess I just felt like you have enough to deal with... I mean..." Suddenly, Emily felt sorry for her teacher. She looked so lost for words. Emily smiled at her. She was positive now that she had not been intentionally left out of anything.

Mrs. Payne looked at her again, very seriously. "Now, Emily, let me try to explain this again. I honestly feel very badly that you are in a wheelchair, and somehow, I just didn't want to put even one more thing on you than you already have to do. I assure you, I thought I was doing you a favor by leaving you out. You have enough to be dealing with... in life.. without adding something... well... relatively unimportant like a play to the mix." She paused. "Do you understand what I'm saying, Emily?"

Emily was starting to feel a little better. "I think so," she said. Her voice was a little more confident now. "But the play *is* important to me."

"I understand that now," said Mrs. Payne. She smiled at Emily reassuringly. Then Mrs. Payne, who was not the hugging type - AT ALL - leaned down and hugged her. "Emily, please know I would *never* do anything to exclude you from anything," she said simply. "And I'm very glad you came to talk to me about this," she added.

She straightened. "See you kids later," she added briskly, turning around and going back towards the stage. Then she stopped and turned back around. She smiled. "Oh, Emily... I'll find a part for you in the show. We will talk tomorrow," she added simply. Then she finished walking to the front of the room, her high heels going "tap-tap-tap!" on the floor.

"Ralph, you are my hero!" teased Emily. "how did you know that would go so well? "

Ralph puffed himself up proudly. Emily laughed. He looked so like a rooster when he did that! Ralph laughed, too. "I just guessed that she wasn't doing it on purpose. I bet," he added, "That the same kind of thing will happen next time too. I don't think people are leaving you out of things on purpose. Maybe you just have to speak up, so they know that you want to be included in the first place."

Emily was silent. She thought there might be something to his words. It was amazing, she thought, how often she had been afraid of something, when it turned out - in the end - that there had been nothing to be frightened of in the first place. She had learned quite a lesson today. And she was glad that she had a friend like Ralph to encourage her to face her fears.

The three friends walked down the hallway together and out the door, where Emily's mom was waiting in the van to take them home.

It was 11 o'clock on Christmas morning. The kids were all gathered in Ralph's living room. Ralph and Sam were playing with Ralph's new LEGO set. Dylan was spinning the blue Beyblade that Mr. O'Mara... Bob... had had gotten him for Christmas. And Emily was reading the new book Ralph had given her. Ruby was perched contentedly on Emily's lap, sleeping soundly, worn out from all of the excitement of Christmas morning. Her new red Christmas collar showed up beautifully against her white fur. And - last but certainly not least - Noodle was curled up on the floor chewing the HUGE bone that had been his Christmas present from Ralph's family. Watching him, Dylan laughed. "It's almost bigger than he is!" he shouted. Noodle seemed to smile at him with twinkling eyes as he continued to worry the bone with his teeth.

Ralph liked his new presents, but the best thing about Christmas was having his mom and dad, his friends, and Noodle and Ruby around him. He looked at his mom and dad sitting on the couch, talking quietly, their arms around each other, with his mom's hand resting on her belly, which it seemed to Ralph got a little bigger every day! He looked at sensitive Emily, with her blue eyes shining, and Dylan, happy at the recent changes in his home life... and he thought that, after all, Christmas was really not all about getting new toys - but Christmas was about love, and family and friends, and helping others.

It had, Ralph that, been a really awesome year. And he couldn't wait for the next one!

Lightning Source UK Ltd.
Milton Keynes UK
UKHW020809130121
376933UK00003B/221